CW01496738

For new and upcoming releases visit

www.kimharryauthor.com

*Back From the Edge*

ISBN: 9781739743215

Published by Pegbag Publishing.

First Printing, 2023

## Dedication

To my good friend Adam Taxiboi Smith.

Thanks for always supporting me

and giving us

Newport Pride 2022

xxx

# Beechwood Estate Series

## Book 3

# BACK FROM THE EDGE

## EDGE

Kim Harry

# PROLOGUE

Late 2011

Reluctantly, Sue Evans stopped at the traffic lights. 'Come on, will you?' She muttered under her breath. She tapped her hand on the side of the steering wheel as if to make them change faster, but as soon as they did, only three cars managed to get through. She looked at her son Jake sitting in the back seat getting frustrated with his hand-held game and she felt like throwing the bloody thing out of the window.

Two cars through this time, and she was next. Hopefully, they would make it to school before the bell. She watched the stream of parents desperately dragging their little ones along the road to the school. Some were in work clothes, some were still in their dressing gowns. That's what she loved about living on the Beechwood estate. It had such a diverse community of characters.

Out of her side window, she noticed a younger woman with striking long, curly, red hair bustling along amongst the many. She looked at herself in the mirror, coiffed her own red hair, and tutted. Ah, who am I trying to kid? She thought. The beep from behind brought her back to reality as the lights turned green and she bolted off, almost stalling the car in the process.

After driving around frantically looking for a space, she wedged the car between the edge of the flats and the last remaining tree. This was the only place she could find to park and still make it to the school on time.

After taking a quick look around for the traffic warden, she joined the flow of humans, like animals, to their watering hole.

Further up the road, she watched as Jean, the daughter of a lady that she cared for, was putting her bin out for collection. She waved to get her attention. The woman reacted instantly and shouted across the street.

'Thanks for the flowers, Sue. My mam loved them.'

'No problem, Jean. How's she doing?'

The woman put her head to the side and gave her a half smile. 'Well, you know. See you on Wednesday, is it?'

Sue gave the same concerned smile back. 'Yeah, I'll be there.'

After more acknowledging nods and waves from the parents approaching in the opposite direction, they made it to the school-gates.

Two smiling teaching assistants were standing on either side of the herd as the more forceful parents pushed their children through.

Sue kissed her son, gave him his bag, and watched as he joined his friends.

As she turned to walk away, a little girl dropped her blue spotty coat, and it distracted her. Sue and the young woman she had noticed earlier both bent down to pick it up. The little girl, with the same beautiful red hair as the woman, smiled, took the coat, and ran through the gates.

'She is beautiful, and her hair is so gorgeous.' Sue looked up at the woman. 'It's just like yours, beautiful. I'd love hair like that.'

The woman smiled. 'Thank you so much. That's so kind of you.'

They stared at each other for a few awkward seconds, then Sue broke the silence. 'Well, must get on. The food won't buy itself.'

With a few tins and a magazine in her shopping basket, Sue continued to browse the shelves. She picked up a large bar of chocolate off the shelf and placed it in the basket. Before it had time to settle amongst the rest of the items, she took it back out again and put it back on the shelf. As she turned to walk away, she changed her mind again and grabbed the bar. This time, it made it all the way to the checkout.

As she waited in line, she noticed the woman from the school at the front of the queue. She waved to get her attention, but she didn't see her. The till on the next aisle opened, so Sue quickly jumped lines and the shop girl began scanning her items. Sue tapped the redhead on the shoulder and commented on her shopping.

'You're in for a good night there, Love. Bottle of wine and asparagus. Supposed to be an aphrodisiac, isn't it?'

The woman stared at her for a few seconds, then burst into tears, and left the shop.

Sue noticed that she hadn't taken her shopping, so explained to the checkout girl that she knew the woman and took it out with hers.

When outside, she could see the woman and called out to her.

'Hang on Love, you forgot your shopping.'

The woman stopped, and Sue hurried up to her.

'Are you OK, Love? I didn't mean to be nosy, never know when to shut my mouth me.'

The woman was still in tears. 'I'm sorry it's just...'

Sue took a clean tissue out of her pocket and gave it to her. She continued. 'My fiancée left me last night.' Sue touched her arm and looked over at the coffee shop across the street. 'Let's go over to the café and have a cuppa. You can tell me all about it.'

The sounds of clattering cups and slurping coffee machines were a welcome break from the silence they were both feeling. Again, Sue made the first move and pulled her chair in tight to the table opposite her newfound friend.

'Right then, let's start again, shall we? I'm Sue, and you are?'

The girl paused for a second, then dropped her shoulders. 'I'm Red, everyone calls me Red.'

Sue smiled 'Then that's what I will call you.'

She reciprocated her smile. Sue took off her coat and placed it on the back of the chair. 'That's better. Tell me to mind my own business, but why would anyone want to leave you and that beautiful girl of yours?'

The colour seemed to drain from Red's face.

'He's evil. He left at 3 am this morning while I was sleeping. My baby begged him not to go, but he just shrugged her off.' She took out a compact mirror and checked her appearance while still talking. 'She came into me screaming that she was sorry, blaming herself for him leaving.'

The waitress brought their coffee to the table and Sue thanked her with a smile. Red seemed agitated that she hadn't kept Sue's undivided attention and raised her voice a little. 'She was always such a daddy's girl, but he's been so horrible to her lately.'

She spooned three sugars into her coffee and stirred the spoon loudly while fixating on Sue's reaction.

'He's always been horrible to me, bringing up my abuse all the time.'

Sue shifted uncomfortably in her chair at the word abuse being mentioned so liberally and whispered her reply. 'That's awful.'

'I just can't have her going through what I went through. I just can't.'

Sue interrupted. 'No, no, I can imagine. The poor little dab.' She blew on her coffee before taking a sip and thought of the girl at the gates. 'She looked so happy this morning, smiling away. Kids are good at hiding their feelings, though, not like us.'

'She shouldn't have to hide anything. My father abused me my entire childhood, and nobody believed me. They still don't.'

'Christ, you poor thing. You must have suffered.'

Red drew back from the table and put her hands on her lap. 'I'm sorry. I shouldn't be burdening you with all this. We've only just met.'

'Don't be daft. You can talk to me anytime. I'm always around.'

Later that evening, Sue was sitting on the end of the bed talking to Dai, her husband, through the mirror of her dressing table whilst hastily applying her night moisturiser.

'Aw, Dai, you should have seen her. I felt terrible. There was nothing I could say to help her.'

Dai answered his wife's reflection. 'You can't fix everyone, Sue. This bloke sounds a bit of a tosser. Just stay out of it. You know what you're like.' He pulled back the quilt for Sue to get in. 'Let them get on with it. They'll probably be back together on the weekend.'

'It's the little girl I feel sorry for. She's a lovely little thing.'

Dai rolled his eyes at her 'That may be the case, Sue, but you can't interfere. Remember last time.'

She knew what he had meant. There had been a time at the school gates when Sue had been standing up to a young girl's partner who she had just seen push her to the floor. She pushed the man back with such force that he cracked his back on the edge of a curb. The police had been involved as the wimp of a man, then wanted to file an assault against Sue. The case was later dropped as Dai paid him off. Sue couldn't have any kind of criminal record in her line of work.

Her doting husband kissed her on the cheek and turned off the light.

The next morning, the traffic was worse than the last time she had made the journey. Late again, Sue was now one of the mothers pushing her son through the school gate, as the sound of the bell echoed through the entrance.

She took a breath and looked around to see if she could see Red. There was no sign of her, so she walked back to her car. It was a beautiful morning, and one she hadn't noticed while rushing her way through the school drop off.

She sat in the car with her eyes closed for a second, enjoying the moment's peace. As she turned the key, she was startled by the banging on the side window. It was Red. Sue wound the window down and smiled.

'Thanks for yesterday, Sue.'

'No problem—don't mention it honestly.'

Red leaned in through the open window. 'Can I repay the favour? I don't have to be at work till 11 am—coffee?'

'Sounds good to me. Get in and I'll drive us there.'


The women sat at what was slowly becoming their usual table, drinking their coffee like old friends.

'So where do you work, Red? You didn't say.'

'I'm a psychiatrist.' Red pushed her hair away from her face. 'So, all over, really. I've been counselling at the Wellview Clinic in town lately, so not far.'

Sue appeared visibly shocked. 'Well, I never. You seem too young to be doing that. My husband, Dai, thinks I'm kooky.' She took a sip of her coffee and wiped the milk from her top lip before continuing. 'I work with cancer patients. You know palliative care ones. Poor buggers, they haven't got long. You never get used to losing them, either. I go home in tears some days.'

Red seemed to show no regard for Sue's words and interrupted her heartfelt speech. 'Everyone says I look too young.' She started dabbing bits of sugar off the table and licking her finger. 'I used my studying as a way of blocking everything out through my teenage years. Then when I met Luke, things went well for me for a while, until...' She paused and seemed to inhale Sue's reaction to her revelations.

'It's OK, you don't have to tell me.'

'No, I want to. It helps, in a strange sort of way. When I told Luke about what my father did, he started asking questions and comparing himself with him. He used to ask me to call him Daddy when we made love. He's sick.'

A police car passed the window, and its loud siren made them both jump. She continued. 'He used to lock me in the bathroom and go out for hours at a time. He used to tell me it was just a game, as he knew how I liked to play little girls' games.'

'I can't believe how much you've been through. I would have fallen to pieces by now. You're better off without him.' Sue looked at the clock behind Red. It was 10.45, and she remembered she said she had to be at work by 11 am. 'Look. Are you at the Wellview Clinic today? Can I drop you off?

Red glanced back at the clock herself and got out of her chair.

'Yes, I am. Thanks, Sue. That would be so helpful.'

Outside the clinic, the women waved their goodbyes. Red walked over to the receptionist, who greeted her knowingly. 'I think you're in room 11 today Red, hang on and I'll take you down.'

Red followed the receptionist down the corridor and knocked on the door before entering.

Dr Sedgewick, a man in his sixties, greeted her whilst still sitting at his desk. There was a large leather chair to the right of him and he ushered the woman to sit down.

'Chloe, how are we feeling today?'

The woman frowned. 'Nobody calls me that anymore. My name is Red. Red Fisher and don't you forget it.' She flounced herself into the chair and seemed flustered. 'Where's Dr Lamb? Off on an expensive holiday again, is she? She needs to be here. My stepfather pays her enough to be here.'

The bearded man moved from his chair and perched himself on the edge of his desk.

'I believe her mother is ill, Chloe. We tried but couldn't contact you in time to explain the situation. So how do you feel now that we have diagnosed a personality disorder?'

'I'm a sociopath. I'm not capable of feeling anything according to fucking Google.' She pulled out her compact mirror from her handbag and checked out her lipstick. 'It's just one step up from a psychopath, I guess.' She started rocking in her chair. 'My stepfather will be pleased. He can tell all his friends at the bank that his stepdaughter has a *condition* instead of excusing me as just a fantasist.'

'I don't think your stepfather sees you as that Chloe. As I understand, both of your parents have been very supportive.'

She gripped the hand rests on the armchair tight, menacingly rocking back and forth.

'There's no need to feel anxious Chloe, let's just chat about you. Can you describe yourself to me?'

A dead stare greeted him.

'What do you like least, or best about yourself?'

'What do you want me to say?' She brushed her hair away from her face suggestively. 'I know you find me attractive. I can see by the way you look at me. So, what do you think my best qualities are?'

'I'm not attracted to you, Chloe. Do you always think that men are attracted to you?'

'My abuser Luke was attracted to me.'

Dr Sedgewick moved back to his desk and picked up a case file.

'Ah, Luke, yes, I read about him in here. He was your stepfather's personal assistant at the bank, yes?'

She stared at him in silence. This old fart had no idea about her life, she thought.

'I thought you'd stopped the allegations made against him after the court cleared him of all charges.' He kept his head buried ignorantly in the file. 'It says here that he provided firm evidence. He was out of the country with his wife when you said that the incident took place.'

She rose from her seat and screamed in his face.

'You know nothing about me.' She paced around the floor before slamming her hand firmly on the desk.

'Look, can I go now? You can tick all the little boxes and tell Stepdaddy I turned up like a good little girl. I just—want—to go.'

The doctor ignored her request and sat back at his desk. 'How's work, Chloe? Do you talk to people there?'

She rolled her eyes at him and sat back down in her chair. 'Of course, I talk to people. It's a fucking call-centre.'

They sat in silence for a few seconds, then a smile appeared across her face. She sat forward in her chair.

'There is this one girl there, Sue. We went for coffee. I think she likes me — well, I think she's stalking me, actually.'

'Do you see this as a productive friendship? Are you open and honest?'

She interrupted his questioning by banging on the arms of the chair. 'Can I go now?' She carried on rhythmically pounding away at the arms until she couldn't handle the situation anymore. 'Why am I asking for your permission? I'm going.'

As she left the room, she made sure that she slammed the door hard enough to make the partition walls shake. She had felt nothing but anger from the session as she stormed into the toilets opposite.

After letting out a scream and pacing the floor, she slammed her head hard down on the shiny white sink. As she brought her head up to look in the mirror, the faint cut above her nose began to ooze with blood.

* * *

The next morning, Sue made sure she was on time. She had a few visits with work lined up, so had rushed through her application form for a new job. She didn't think that she had a chance of getting it, but would try all the same.

Dai had asked her to go to the bank and draw out three hundred pounds for him to pay off his car repairs. She had spent ages last night looking for her passport to use as proof of identity, just to make sure she wasn't late this morning.

She kissed Jake's head as he went through the gates and made her way to the High Street.

Red was following her from behind, on the other side of the road. The chiffon scarf that was covering her face was getting tangled around her red curls.

Before Sue came out of the bank, she shoved the money into the envelope with the rest of her important documents. She had managed to get a space not far from the school and was pleased with herself that she had done what she had intended to do.

After driving for a few metres, she slammed down the brakes, hitting her chest hard against the steering wheel, as a distraught Red had stepped off the kerb in front of her. She hoped to God that she hadn't hit the woman and shakily made her way out of the car.

'I'm so sorry, I didn't see you. Are you OK?'

The chiffon scarf had strategically dropped away from Red's face, leaving the cut on her nose and the two black eyes that had now developed, visible. She hesitantly covered it back up, just leaving it long enough to have its desired effect on Sue.

'Oh, my God. What's happened? That wasn't me, was it?'

She held Red by the elbow and helped to steady her.

'It was Luke, I—I couldn't stop him.'

The fake tears fell and, whilst appearing off balance, she fell into Sue's arms.

She maneuvered Red's body into the front seat, then jumped into the driver's side to start the engine. 'Right, I'm taking you to the police station. He can't get away with this.'

Red stopped Sue from driving by putting her hand across the wheel. 'No, please stop. I can't. He told me that if I ever go to the police, he will take her from me, and I will never see her again. He has a lot of friends at the police force.'

Sue went into her bag and got Red a tissue. 'But you should report it, my lovely.'

This made Red appear even more distraught. 'No, he'd kill me. He told me to come straight home after dropping her at school.'

Sue tried to calm her down. She was desperate to find another solution. 'OK, OK. Is there somewhere you can go? Friends or family?'

Red shook her head. 'I'm not from around here. Everyone I trust is over four hundred miles away. He's taken my phone, emptied the bank account, and everything is gone. We're trapped here.' She paused as if to gather her thoughts, then screamed at the top of her lungs. 'I can't go back there—I can't.'

Sue rubbed her back as she sat arched over crying.

'Listen, it will be OK.' She reached for the envelope that had the money in it and gave it to Red.

'Go and get your girl from the school and take her as far away as you can possibly get. If I hadn't had my ladies to see this morning, I would take you myself.'

Red stared at Sue. This was something she wasn't expecting, and, for one single moment, she thought that she felt an ounce of guilt. It was short-lived. As soon as she saw the wad of notes nestled in the envelope, the tears she forced out were mainly from joy.

'I'll pay you back, Sue. As soon as we are away from here, I'll get that money back to you. I promise.'

'You can't risk it when kids are involved. Go now when you've got the chance.'

* * *

Sue tried to put the morning's incidents out of her head as she cared for her patient. She poured the hot soapy water down the sink and rinsed out the bowl she had used to give Jean's mum her bed bath. The old lady had lost her speech, but she did still manage a smile.

'Aw, she looks a lot more comfortable now, thanks, Sue.' Jean walked over to her mother's bedside and stroked her mother's hair whilst staring aimlessly into space. She bent down and kissed the top of her head as the old lady patted her hand.

'Fed, watered and a bath. You've been spoiled today, Mum.'

Sue ripped the plastic apron off her neck and rolled it into a ball before putting it in the bin with her plastic gloves. She gave her hands a quick swill and joined Jean in the living room. She grabbed her coat from the edge of the bed and checked on the lady a final time.

'I think she looks a lot brighter today, Jean. Try to get some rest when she does, and make sure you both eat something later, OK. I'll be checking up on you.' She put her coat on and hugged Jean. 'I best get going, as Jake will be out of school soon.'

She closed the front door behind her and crossed the road to the school. Some parents were already leaving the school with their kids in tow. Sue joined her son's friend's mum Carol. The boys had been friends since nursery and were always in and out of each other's houses.

'Hey, Sue. Glad I caught you. Is it OK if Jake comes over for his tea tonight? Billy is having trouble with his new game, and he said that Jake is fantastic on it.'

'Yeah, no problem, Love. I'll just wait and say hi, then I'll get off.'

'I'll drop him back later if that's OK?'

The two boys came out together and Sue saw the three of them off with a mother's hug. As she turned to leave, she noticed the little girl with her beautiful red hair being picked up by a stern-looking man.

She waved her hands frantically above her head to get the teaching assistants' attention as he was standing next to them. He saw her mouth, something at him, but couldn't grasp what she was saying.

She hurried towards them, pushing her way through the sea of irate parents, and managed to get close enough to be heard.

'He's not supposed to take her. Her mother said he's not supposed to take her.'

She pointed at the man and the girl, who were now afraid of all the shouting. Holding on tightly to the man's leg, she turned in toward him.

The crowd of parents were now circling the commotion and staring at the man. He, too, was feeling intimidated and confused. The teaching assistant tried to disperse the crowd and took Sue to one side.

'What seems to be the problem here?'

'He's not supposed to take her. That man has beaten her mother, and she is in a terrible state. He's nothing but a bully.'

The young man looked around and tried to take stock of the situation.

'This is Cerys's father, and her mother is standing by her car over there. There must be some mistake, Mrs Evans.'

Sue looked over to the car opposite, which had a woman standing outside of it, raising her hands with upturned palms, wondering what was going on. Sue didn't recognise the woman and argued in front of the watching crowd.

'That is not the girl's mother. I'm telling you; something is not right here.'

The girl started crying, and a few of the mothers that knew Sue came over to see if they could help. The teaching assistant insisted that they take the commotion inside. Sue agreed and was questioned by the head of the school that had known Sue for a long time.

'Mrs Evans, I assure you that these people are who they say they are. Cerys hasn't been with us for very long and I have had meetings with both of her parents several times when they were considering sending her here. Are you sure you have the right girl?'

Sue looked down at Cerys. She had the right girl as she recognised the blue spotty coat she was wearing when she first saw her at the gates. Her mind was so confused. She made her apologies to all concerned and left embarrassed by her conduct.

Sue decided to drive to the Wellview clinic, hoping to get an address for Red. Something must have gone horribly wrong, and this worried her. She couldn't shake the feeling that her new friend was in trouble.

She approached the receptionist and asked if she knew of a psychiatrist that had been working there by the name of Red. The receptionist looked a little confused. They had a patient visiting there by that name, but she couldn't tell Sue that, due to patient confidentiality. She suggested to Sue that she wait while she called one of the doctors. Sue declined. She needed to think, so left the building to return home.

Each time she had seen Red, there had been something that didn't feel right, but she didn't expect any deceit. The realisation that she may have been conned, began to eat away at her. Not only was she feeling stupid, but would have to face telling her husband that she had given away his hard-earned cash.

When Dai came through the door, Sue was in the kitchen, hovering around a boiling kettle. He shouted from the living room at her, but she didn't answer.

'Sue, did you manage to get that money out for me?'

She didn't answer at first because she had tried to avoid the question. But after Dai asked a second time, she had to respond. 'No sorry Love, time just flew by so fast today. I'll try to get over there tomorrow.'

Sue knew that lying wasn't the answer, but she had felt such a fool for being taken in by this con woman. She had given herself more credit than that. If she could give herself another day, she was certain that she could find the woman and convince her to give it back, but didn't know where to start.

The next day, she spent the morning scouring the streets in her car. Looking in shop windows to see if she could get a glimpse of the woman that had taken her for a mug had given no success.

After finally giving up, she went to the bank and used her old credit cards to withdraw three hundred pounds to give to Dai. God knows how she would make the payments every month, as Dai knew exactly what was coming in and going out of the account, she thought.

The credit cards were only in her name. When Dai had been having trouble getting credit, they had used them to get them out of a temporary situation, so hopefully, this would work.

In a desperate attempt to find the woman, she drove into the next town's High Street, hoping she may get lucky. The pub on the corner had an advert in the window for a pot-washer, so she thought she'd enquire. If it was night work, she could tell Dai that she was visiting a patient who was close to the end of life. He had a heart of gold and would understand if she was needed. She hated lying to him, but could see no other way out. The situation was already way out of hand. She would try anything to put it right.

Chapter One

2001

Things were different when Ruby and her family left the Beechwood estate with the new stepfather, moving them to a more affluent part of Newport.

Chloe Fisher had lost her only loyal friend. She had waited for a letter or an invitation for a playdate, but it never came. She had simply been forgotten. Her mafia boss wannabe father, the notorious Frankie Thompson, was now in prison, and things had been quiet around the house for a while.

At school, the other kid's parents still looked down their noses at her. She was the eleven-year-old daughter of a drug dealing bully that had tainted the estate by getting their kids hooked on anything they could afford. It was the ones that couldn't afford the stuff that had been the worst off. Frankie had reeled these in with his freebies and then put them out to work for him. When they were hooked, he would take away the free candy and make them pay for it by using them as runners. They would scowl around the estate with their hoodies pulled down, hiding their faces, when collecting money and delivering drugs.

Chloe learned to hold her own and act like the hard chip off the old block when it came to the beatings. And as she began to grow, so did her confidence. She wasn't going to stand for it anymore and became feared by a lot of the kids, as her outbursts were too dangerous. Chloe refused to let the teachers control her, and her mother was too focused on finding a new husband to pay attention to what was happening to Chloe.

'The thing is, Miss Fisher, I know your daughter has had a lot to deal with, but she can't take it out on the other children. They are all afraid of her. She has these... shall we say, temper tantrums, and for no particular reason, it seems. She throws tables around and damages school property. It is just not acceptable.'

When Chloe was suspended for the last time at thirteen, she used her free time to travel across town to locate Ruby. She had found out the address a while back, from the new neighbours that were living in her old house. They had used it to forward mail. Ruby was the only chance she had of ever having a friend. They had shared secrets that were too vile for anyone else's ears.

As she approached the house, she saw Ruby looking at her through the window. Her stomach jolted in anticipation as she walked up the path. Ruby opened the door before Chloe had the chance to knock. Chloe smiled, for the first time in a long time, at her old friend. Over a year had passed, and she had played out this moment many times in her young mind. The smile, unfortunately, was not reciprocated. The blank expression she received from Ruby was the same as the ones she had received many times from the other kids at the school.

'Ruby, it's me.'

The girl stared at her for a while, then replied, 'Sorry, I don't know who you are. We are not giving to charity today.'

The door was then shut firmly behind her.
With a heavy heart and the knowledge that she was truly alone, she vowed never to put her trust in anyone again.

Her mother, Joan, had finally met someone daft enough to take on Frankie Thompson's leftovers. He was from Cardiff and hadn't heard of the Thompson family's reputation. Joan Fisher was leaving the estate at last. She had no marital ties to Frankie, as he hadn't even bothered to put a ring on her finger. Anyway, he was still locked up, but she was a free woman to marry whomever she felt fit.

She had only been a slip of a girl when she became Frankie's bit on the side and had only started seeing him, as he liked to flash his cash. He had a wife and two wayward sons at home, but he had promised that he would leave them behind for her if she stayed on his arm.

When Joan fell pregnant, he stayed true to his word and bought them a house on the estate. He paid for it outright in cash. But later on, the bubble burst, and he was now doing time at her majesty's pleasure.

Joan was beside herself to have found herself a man such as Brian Stanley. He wasn't what you would call a looker, but he had cash to spend, so that was good enough for her.

After the wedding, Brian insisted that Chloe was to call him Father. After all, he was the one that had bribed the head teacher of the girls' boarding school at St Hilda's to take in the unruly Chloe Fisher. This was Brian's way.

If he couldn't fix a problem, he would throw money at it to make it go away. He couldn't keep any control over Chloe, so she had to go.

St Hilda's was full of spoilt, over-privileged kids that didn't give a shit about rules or the rule makers. You would think that Chloe would fit in with this regime, but the treatment she got from these kids was worse than the ones on the estate. She simply didn't fit in with any of the types that flounced the halls of St Hilda's. Her look was too natural with her flowing unkempt hair and her old kicker boots, which she refused to part with. They all took the piss out of her accent, too. It was too chavvy for them to understand.

Chloe was alone again. This was fine by her until the bullying started. At her old school, she could rely on her family's reputation as well as her mouth to do the work for her, but here was different. They would come at her in the middle of the night in gangs of at least six. Pulling the bedcovers over her head and punching the crap out of her body restricted her. She didn't stand a chance.

Fiona, the head of the in-crowd, was the one who everyone went to if they needed a fix. It was common knowledge that the girl was having trouble with her supplier, so Chloe thought that this may be, her way in.

She still had contact with her brothers, as whenever they needed money, they would come crawling around their forgotten little sister for a handout. As if she had any to give.

She saved any money she could steal in a sock in her bottom drawer. If she could get them to sort out a regular supply, she could get the bullies to leave her alone.

'The thing is Sis, I would help you out, but Dad has to oversee everything. He said if you go to see him in the nick, he will sort it out for you.'

Typical. He was still pulling all the strings from inside. She hated him. The only reason he would have wanted her there would be for his benefit, and she knew it.

'Why? Can't he just sort it out for me? He owes me that much, at least.'

When Wayne contacted Frankie about Chloe's predicament, he saw it as a way to show the new governor of the prison that he was a family man. That meant if there was any chance of parole, he would use his newfound status for a bit of leverage. He couldn't remember the girl's name half the time, let alone help her out with something that didn't concern him.

There was no way that Chloe would ever want to spend time in his company again. 'Just tell him that this girl is loaded. She's not one of his little estate suppliers. These kids in here have got hundreds in pocket money to shove up their noses.'

Wayne managed to change Frankie's mind, and a deal was made.

For the rest of her time at St. Hilda's, Chloe had not only been left alone by the bullies after her father's name was mentioned but they had also protected her from the hassle of anyone else.

Her time was now spent totally alone. She was able to get into her own shit of stealing from the teachers while spiralling downwards into a mental breakdown with added self-abuse. Nobody knew, as she kept her cutting to herself. Hidden from judging eyes. Not that anyone would give a shit, anyway.

When she left school at sixteen, Brian came to her with a list of how he wanted her to run her life. He had found her a job and a flat that was just far enough from them that she couldn't pop in to see her mother every day.

She had told him how much of a wanker she thought he was, in his big bank manager chair. She would ride her bike down to his office and sit in the waiting room just to annoy him. His personal assistant Luke had kicked her out with sympathy so many times that they had become almost friends.

The final Monday that she came into his office, she made sure that Luke wasn't there. He didn't deserve to witness this kind of shit, she thought.

Chloe entered the waiting room safely tucked behind a random couple and then made her way to the corner seat by the window. After acting on her release, she watched as the blood dripped down from her wrists, off the arms of the chair and onto the cream-coloured carpet. Each drip pounded in her brain as she slowly fell into a deep sleep of unconsciousness.

When she finally awoke, the fog had lifted. At first, the white walls around her made her feel like she was in heaven, or on a higher plane at least. It was only when she heard the jabbering of the nurses that she realised where she was. She had failed. Her attempt to be the one that got away had failed. As she lay there, she evaluated her life. There had to be more than this, she thought. She was only eighteen.

The nurses rallied around her when they realised that she was awake.

'When will I be able to go home?'

They smiled at her as if to say we have no answers and carried on remaking her bed with her in it. A man in a suit was the next to visit.

'Hello Miss Fisher, I'm Mr Sands. Your father has sent me to take a look at you.'

'Frankie... he's out? Fuck, how long have I been asleep?'

The man looked confused and put her reaction down to delirium.

'Your father, Brian Stanley, has instructed me to...'

She interrupted him. 'He's not my father, you daft prick. He's the twat my mother married.'

The man looked confused. 'Well anyway, Chloe, do you know where you are?'

She looked around with eyes open wide. 'I'd take a wild guess and say that I was in the hospital.' she looked at the man as if he was an idiot.

'This is a psychiatric hospital, Chloe. You are here because you tried to take your own life.'

She had remembered that much. She had been feeling like shit all week. She had tried to talk to her mam about how she was feeling, but she had been too wrapped up in herself and Brian, as always. That was why she had chosen his office to do it in. He had taken her mother away from her so he would pay in blood.

'Your father,' he corrected himself, 'Mr Stanley has booked you into the hospital to get some therapy. Your injuries were quite severe, and as far as I can gather, you have been suffering with your mental health for quite some time. He has kindly offered to put himself forward as your power of attorney. It appears that you have run up a lot of bills and may face eviction from your property. Mr Stanley has taken legal advice and is now helping you out of the rut you had got yourself into.'

This was because Brian had got her into a flat that she couldn't afford. If he had let her stay at home with them, she would never have gotten into debt in the first place.

'So, what are you trying to say here, Doc? I'm now in the loony bin and my so-called stepfather Brian has taken my rights away?'

'I wouldn't put it quite like that, Miss Fisher. It seems he has just taken care of things for you.'

How fucking dare he, she thought. She was in this mess because of him. He knew how unstable she was, and she had begged her mother to let her come and live with them. This was her third suicide attempt this year. She would admit that the others had been to get the attention of her mother to wake her up to her plea. But this time, she had had enough. She wanted to die. No fucker cared, not even her mother. She would be sorry, she thought. If the police did some digging on why, a young girl would want to take her own life.

As the doctor continued to spout on about her rights, Chloe switched off. Why should she listen? The Chloe they were talking about had been taken over by the mental health board. The new Chloe that she had now felt determined she would be to be was nobody's puppet. She would get herself together and get out of this place. The knowledge that bloody Brian practically owned her was too much to bare. She was Chloe Fisher. Daughter of the notorious Frankie Thompson. She may have hated the bastard, but she knew that she had some of his fire in her belly. She wasn't going to let them drug her up to the eyeballs on antidepressants. This was the kick that she had needed.

For the next few years, she went from job to job, from scam to scam. Her father was released from prison, and she had heard from her beloved family members that he was up to his old tricks. For once, she was glad that Brian had taken her mother off the estate. She remembered what it was like having him around. At least now, though, she was big enough to have been able to push him off when he tried to climb into bed with her every night. She hated the bastard. She knew that if she ever mentioned his sick ways to anyone, she would be dead. He had told her as much. She had seen first-hand when she was ten years old what happens to anyone that crosses the notorious Frankie Thompson.

She had been sitting in her bedroom playing with her dolls when she saw her father dragging a fourteen-year-old boy across the car park by his foot. She lost sight of them for a second, then heard an almighty crash as he swung him up over his head and threw him with full force on top of her playhouse. The boy was small for his age and tried to kick him off as he forced him down onto the floor. Chloe stopped watching after that. The disturbance was deafening, and she couldn't hear her little tape player. She turned it right up, but even the cheerful sound of S Club 7 couldn't drown out the screams of pain from the boy.

When she went out in the garden the next day, she noticed blood and ripped clothing amongst her garden play toys. Her young imagination wouldn't let her accept what horror the boy may have faced, and she played amongst her toys in ignorance.

She wasn't going to get in contact with him and she was damn sure that he would want nothing to do with the adult Chloe Fisher.

As time went on, she was starting to forget about him. Life wasn't too bad. She had held down a job for longer than a month, and the nightmares had lessened.

This all changed when Chloe had a visit from the police. Her father was dead. Jack had shot him. And she had shed not a single tear.

* * *

The hearse carrying Frankie's body had arrived at the social club of the Beechwood estate. Most of the crowd had only turned up to make sure he was dead. For years, he had been a bad influence on the estate, getting the kids into drugs, and then using them as runners to pay off their dues. Not anymore. After Jack found out that he had abused his sister when she was small, he couldn't control his anger. He shot Frankie, then shot himself.

A young, clean-shaven man stepped out in front of the crowd in funeral attire. He held his fist to his mouth, then coughed rather loud to demand the attention of the so-called mourners. With his hands now solemnly locked in front of him, he spoke.

'As you all know, Frankie was a pillar of the community. His passing was a shock to us all.'

The professional mourner that they had hired to celebrate Frankie's life had not done his homework. The crowd stood with looks of confusion as he carried on with the eulogy of an entirely different man. Not the sadistic bastard that was Frankie Thompson.

A sea of burly men in black coats filled the church car park. Each one had tried to get a space at the front as the hearse reached its final destination. Whether they were there out of loyalty or the need to be seen by others remained a mystery. Most of Frankie's men had been sent down for their involvement in the counterfeit money racket that Frankie had been running.

The little family he had left comprised of aged aunts on his mothers' side. They were all in their 90's and refusing to die. The tittle-tattle amongst them made it obvious that they were only there for the buffet.

The funeral director was doing his best to keep an orderly flow of cars and mourners onto the church grounds. He'd been attentive to the fact that there was also a police presence.

'Don't park there,' he shouted to Chloe, who had dressed casually in jeans and a t-shirt.

'If you're delivering flowers, you need to take them in through the back door.'

Not impressed by his curt manner, she scowled at him before moving to the back entrance.

The crowd split down the middle as the bearers carried his solid oak coffin into the church. Behind them, with his head slightly bowed, was his son, Wayne Thompson. He shared a pair of handcuffs with a prison guard. They had allowed him out for the service, but he would not be attending a wake of any kind afterwards. Kevin Thompson, Frankie's other son, had kept his distance. The feud in the family had continued. Kevin was gay and Frankie had disowned him for it.

The funeral had its usual array of hymns and fake tears. Even the vicar, it seemed, had been gently persuaded to only say nice things about the man, before giving his final blessing.

As he doused the coffin with the sign of a cross, the dragging of the large wooden doors being opened inwards behind him disturbed him.

Walking down the aisle like a jilted bride, his estranged daughter Chloe sauntered up to the pulpit. She trailed her fingers along Frankie's coffin, then bent down and kissed it. This was then followed by an almighty scream which had the funeral bearers coming to her side to comfort her.

After shaking them off, she turned to the coffin one last time and spat over the brass plaque.

The crowd reacted. Some were shocked, and some wished that they had had the balls to do it themselves.

Chloe was escorted back down the aisle, with a bearer on either side.

Before leaving the building, she shook off her captors and turned to face the mourners one more time. She raised her middle finger and shouted at the top of her lungs. 'Fuck you, Daddy.'

Chapter Two

Present day 2013

'Lola, Moose, you're lying on my jacket. Come on, guys. Down!'

'They're not listening to you, Heather. They don't want you to leave either. I'm sure the station can do without you for just one more hour. It can't be that important. Come back to bed.'

Martha's eyes had that encouraging look about them. Heather had already turned down the overtime at the weekend to spend quality time at the beach house with her. But, she had had to cut it short, as the chief had called her in especially. She would be walking into something heavy, she could feel it.

Heaving, she pushed the Labradors to the side of the ottoman and pulled out a rather crumpled hairy jacket by her fingertips. She attempted to brush it off, then, mindful of the time, gave up, swinging it around her shoulders in a cloud of canine fur.

Martha was still in a heap under the covers on the bed that they had spent most of the weekend on. With a gleeful eye, Heather managed to open the cocoon to give her a quick kiss before leaving. Martha responded with one eye closed.

'Wait a minute. Is that all I'm getting? At least let me make you some breakfast?'

Heather turned away and headed for the door. 'Call me!' Martha hollered, as the door shut firmly behind her.

The station was looking as busy as ever when she walked through. The team that she was working with wasn't the best, and she still hadn't bonded with many.

Most of them knew her as the cop turned lesbian that used to be married to DI Gareth Williams. Even though she was also a DI, her rank hadn't been as respected as his.

She could hear familiar voices as she approached the incident room and slowed her pace to work out what they were saying.

'I'm telling you, that girl has a problem. Ever since she got with Martha and started flying the LGBT flag, she can't keep her mind on the job.'

'Ah, jealousy is a lonely word. Anyone would think you were after her job, Detective Bennet.'

He shrugged off the comment. Although, he was convinced that he could do a better job than any woman. Even those that were working their way up the ranks.

'No, that's not the case one bit, Shane. When she was married to Gareth, she always did overtime. All I'm saying is, if he was still around, I think she would be back to her old self.'

The fact that Gareth had taken a transfer instead of Heather had peeved a lot of them off. He had left her to defend herself as the one that was having the affair.

Gareth and Heather had shared an open bisexual marriage and had both consented to leave the marriage to be with their new partners. This wasn't common knowledge though, so it was easy to blame the one that was left behind.

'Josh, he's only moved to another station. It's not the other side of the world. They're still good friends, too.

Did you ever think that now she's open about her sexuality, she may not think that she has to prove herself anymore? Anyway, how much overtime have you put in lately? Since you started seeing that girl from admin?'

'Point taken, I suppose.'

Heather was fed up with listening to them. Deciding to be openly lesbian at the station was not her choice. When Martha was attacked, she visibly made her feelings for the woman common knowledge with the amount of distress she was in. She had practically nursed her back from the edge and the rest of the station had watched her every move.

She slowly got closer to their desks and knew that if she kept on listening, it may get worse, so she made her appearance known.

DI Shane Woods noticed her first and started shuffling papers around. He tried to get Bennett's attention to stop him from saying more, but he didn't get the message until she was right behind him. He was startled by the sound of her voice and jumped on his keyboard.

'What's up with you two? You haven't been slagging me off again to the Chief, have you? Eyes and ears in the back of my head, me boys'.

A visible shade of red came over the detectives.

'So, why have we been called into the incident room? Is this about the money going missing?'

The station had been made aware by several of the relatives of the Sunnyville Retirement Home that money had gone missing from their loved ones' accounts along with pieces of jewellery. They hadn't been able to accuse anyone of anything just yet, but they had a few likely suspects in mind.

The manager had said that the staff turnaround was quite frequent as the pay wasn't the best and no one liked the night shifts. They were relying on the CCTV footage around the card machine withdrawals, but as they had taken the money out in corner shops with no CCTV they had hit a wall.

Chief Inspector Morris quietened the room before he began to speak. 'OK, you lot. Thanks for coming in. I know that some of you still had leave left owing, but this is important.' He put on his glasses and tried to make sense of his scribbled notes.

'So, we've just been informed that one of the residents that had had money taken from his account was found dead on Tuesday morning. Apparently, at first, it looked like natural causes, so no need for any police intervention. After further examination by the coroner, they noticed that there was a tooth mark on the inside of his lip and other evidence that suggests he may have been smothered, assumingly with a pillow. The old guy's ribs had also been broken so they're assuming someone was leaning or sitting on his chest.' He put his glasses back into his pocket. 'We need to find out if this is connected with the money theft, so I want you all to make some calls to the relatives. Thank you.'

As the chattering started back up again. The chief waved Heather over. 'Thanks for coming in, Heather. I know it's not your shift.'

'That's OK Chief, I didn't have anything special planned.'

'I want you to go to Sunnyville and get a feel of the place. Find out if he had any arguments with other residents or the staff there, for that matter. And take Shane with you. He could do with having a bit of a reality check on how other people live. I heard him say earlier *how do we know that they hadn't taken the money out themselves?* The daft pratt.'

That was Shane all over, she thought, opening his mouth without thinking it through.

* * *

Retired from the police force, Martha pottered around the house. It was all she seemed to be able to do after being attacked again. This time though, she had had Heather to help her through it.

She still hadn't adjusted to being in a full-time relationship with her, though. Monogamy was new to her.

Now that her time with the force had come to an end, she didn't have much eye candy to swoon over, so it had been easier to kerb her wandering ways. She had wondered whether she had found love with Heather. After all the one-night stands she had shared with her when she was married to Gareth, she had always hoped that there would be a time when they would spend their lives together, and this was now.

She still hadn't asked her to move in with her though. And she had the feeling that Heather didn't want her to, anyway. Could they still be this much in love and live apart? Or should she bite the bullet and ask her to move in? she thought.

Gareth had moved on and had left the station with Matt Reid. The relationship didn't last long, but he seemed happy to be living a single life as a gay man, and they had all remained friends.

It had been a year since Heather and Martha had decided to become exclusive. After Martha's recovery, they were at it like rabbits. They couldn't get enough of each other. But the fizz had now died down. Martha was a little worried that this would happen. This was one of the reasons she didn't do relationships. She got bored easily and wasn't afraid to admit it. Especially to Heather, as she had done in the past. The affair she had with her just before she married Gareth had come close to stopping the marriage. But she couldn't commit. This weekend had been good though. They had had a few weeks' break from each other, and it had made all the difference. The sex felt new and exciting, just like old times. Martha knew that if she could get something to occupy her mind, she wouldn't dwell on things as much. She was jealous of Heather going to the station every day though and had craved the excitement that a fresh case would bring.

* * *

As they arrived at Sunnyville, the sun was shining. Residents were being pushed around the grounds in wheelchairs or helped along by metal zimmer frames. The place had a relaxing feeling about it.

Shane thought of himself as a bit of a comedian. He couldn't help having a dig at someone if the time was right. 'That will be you one day, Heather, pushing Martha along in her chair while she fires her orders at you.'

Heather ignored the comment. Yes, there was an age gap, but Martha had more life in her than half of the blokes at the station.

Shane was always tired. He had two small kids and a wife that really could use more help with them at home.

He was always up for overtime though and told his wife it was compulsory.

Sunnyville was your typical care home. A lot of the residents had Alzheimer's and were suffering from dementia. An average day would see them paraded in a circle, waiting for relatives to make the effort to come and see them.

Some of the more verbal residents were more popular than others. Their relatives were still regularly visiting. Others had succumbed to the horrible disease and had had most of their character taken away. These were the residents with the least visitors. Their loved ones had preferred to remember them how they once were. Finding it too hard to cope with, so had given up on visiting. These were the ones staring at the empty doorways. Secretly wishing for an interaction of any kind.

The manager, Helen Rees, showed the detectives around the place. She was a cheery soul and always acknowledged the residents as she passed them with nods and the odd, caring touch on the arm.

Everyone seemed to be doing their jobs with a high standard of care. The detectives didn't notice anything that looked out of the ordinary.

'Is it OK if we take a look at the room that the resident passed away in please Mrs Rees?'

The woman acknowledged the request and left to get the keys.

As Heather waited, she felt a pull on her hand from an old man in a chair.

'Can I help you, sir?'

The man smiled and dropped his top set of teeth to the bottom. He pulled Heather down to his level and grabbed at her breast.

'Now, now Bill. We don't have any of that in here, do we?' A female carer noticed his actions and grabbed the handles on the back of his chair to pull him away.

'Sorry about that Miss. You should have been told not to get too close to our Bill.'

Heather was a little startled, but this was nothing more than a lot of the old drunks had attempted when she was back in her PC days. Heather followed the carer as she moved Bill to a side room.

'So sorry, it was my fault really. I should have been more on guard.'

The woman laughed and kicked out her foot to put the brakes on. 'On guard 24/7 in this place, unfortunately. We have a few residents that like to wind up the girls by knocking things to the floor so they can get a quick perv. Bill is quite well-behaved compared to some. We used to have a resident that liked to get his old boy out and flash it to the female residents early morning. It would put them off their breakfasts, the poor loves.'

Shane smirked at this, and Heather showed her disapproval of his actions. 'Go and see if she's found the key yet. She seems to be taking her time.'

When he left, she asked the carer if she could have a quiet word and pulled her to one side.

'So, off the record, is this a good place to work?'

The woman looked around to check that she wasn't being overheard. 'Sometimes yes. We have a lot of staff turnarounds, though. No one likes the hours you see. I've been here for fifteen years as it's only me and my old man at home. A lot of the younger ones can't cope with the mess either, you know, so they try it for a couple of weeks, then leave.'

'Fifteen years, wow. You must have seen a few faces come and go then. Did you have much to do with Les Thomas, who's just passed?'

'I did when he first came here, but not since dementia set in. He was a beater—sorry, that's the name we give to the residents that lash out at you. They are all smiles one minute, then will give you a swipe across the back with a walking stick when you're not looking.'

Heather knew the type only too well. Again, she had seen a few of them over the years in the cells. All smiles and charms when you are telling them what they want to hear, then a quick attempt at a slap when you've turned your back.

'So was Les Thomas here long?'

'Yeah, I should say so. When he first arrived, he was quite with it. To be honest, we wondered why he was here. He had enough money and a nice big house. She could have quite easily afforded carers for him.'

'She? As in his family?'

'Yes, he has a daughter. Between you and me, I think she put him in here to ease her load rather than the other way around. He'd had a heart attack, and they had diagnosed him with cardiovascular disease, but he'd recovered well from that. It was nothing that couldn't be monitored.'

She called out for one of the male carers to help Bill into his chair. Then wheeled the wheelchair back into the corridor.

'They diagnosed Les Thomas with Alzheimer's disease about two years later. The poor bugger found it so frustrating when it affected his speech.' She closed Bill's door, then looked at her watch. 'Well, I have to get on. Short staffed again.'

Heather walked down the corridor to where the manager and Shane were waiting for her.

'Are you ready to see the room now, Detective? I don't know what more you will find. Your team has already been over it.'

The room looked pretty much the same as old Bill's room. Only the window hadn't been set on a wedge lock like Bill's. It was free to open.

'Was this window in lock mode when Mr Thomas was in here, Mrs Rees?'

'Oh yes, I'm sure it was. Maybe one of the team released it. We don't normally move the latches as the residents have a habit of getting too close to falling.'

The room was south facing with plenty of sun streaming in. It overlooked a paved visiting area that had undercover circular seating accessed by a ramp. She commented on how beautiful the flowers were in the garden before scanning the room once more.

There was a painting on the wall of a woman in a long red coat smiling at a cat in a garden. And on the bedside table was a photo of a stern-looking woman, without a smile. The rest of the walls were bare. Other than a patient description post, that was taped on the back of the door about Les Thomas.

'May I ask what the other residents thought of Mr Thomas? In your opinion obviously. I'm just trying to grasp a bit about his character.'

'Not a lot, really. He wasn't the type to get involved in any of the day care activities. He used to like being wheeled down to the local shop to buy humbugs, but unfortunately, as his behaviour was so unpredictable, it was hard to get a member of staff that would be comfortable taking him. We would have to release two members of staff if that was the case, and we couldn't always do this.'

'Did his daughter ever take him out?'

'No, sadly. Relatives do sometimes help out but this wasn't the case with Les Thomas. His daughter felt that we should provide all care, and she made a point of making this so.' She had regretted mentioning the daughter as soon as she had said it and hoped that the daughter wouldn't have been told about this.

'I do understand. It must be really hard running a place like this. With its unpredictability, like you said. Can you give me a list of the staff that had spent the most time with Mr Thomas, especially the ones that took him to the shop?'

Helen Rees had to think for a moment. 'Um, there was only one really, and she left the night before he died. As I said nobody else would take him.'

The woman was visibly perturbed. She didn't want Heather to think that they hadn't provided their best care for him. They were paid a great deal of money to look after these residents and their well-being was supposed to be catered for.

'Mrs Rees, I'm not accusing you of not looking after the residents. I just need a list of staff that had contact with Mr Thomas. And as soon as possible, please. You can drop it in at the station or I can send someone to pick it up.'

The woman nodded, and as they left the room, she re-locked the door with a shaky hand.

As they walked away, Shane offered his view of the situation. 'What do you think then Heather? She seems OK. The place didn't smell like old piss and faggots like some of the homes I've been in.'

'Well, that's one way to put it, Detective. But I know what you mean. She did seem like she was under pressure from the daughter, though. Did you see the way she shuffled about when we talked about his well-being? She's been told to dot the I's and cross the T's you can tell.'

Kate, Mr Thomas's daughter, was a receptionist at the doctors' surgery. When patients would ring in to speak to the doctor, they would have to pass vigorous testing from her before she would even consider them for an appointment, let alone be pencilled in with a time slot. She wore high-bowed blouses and overpriced shoes. When the news of her father's death was announced, she immediately called the bank to stop any further payments being made to Sunnyville. This was not the grieving doting daughter that she had led everyone to believe.

Heather decided that they should visit her before making any other assumptions about her.

'Should we be turning up to her place of work unannounced, Heather? If she's a bit of a stickler for protocol.'

'Wait in the car if you're afraid of her, Detective. I can handle this.'

Shane Woods leaned back in his chair and closed his eyes. He didn't need to be asked twice to bow out of a visit with an irate woman. He had been married to one for long enough, so didn't need any more reminders of his incompetence.

'Hi, Miss Thomas. I'm Detective Williams. Is there any chance I can have a quick chat with you somewhere quiet? I have a few questions that I need you to answer for me.'

The woman held her hand out to stop any more speech from Heather, then held it over the mouthpiece.

'Can't you see that I have a phone to my ear, Detective? You will just have to wait.'

It was obvious to all that there was no-one on the other end of the line and that she was on hold or something. But Heather waited. With the odd tap of her foot, she waited.

After a few choice words to whoever it was on the end of the line, she slammed the phone down on to its receiver.

'What can I do for you, Detective? As you can see, I'm a very busy woman.'

'I want to talk to you about your father's murder, Miss Thomas. Would you like me to discuss this here with everyone listening of will you come out from behind that desk and answer my questions?'

The woman looked at her with peeled eyes. She scraped her chair away and mumbled in the ear of the young receptionist, who was sitting in the seat next to her.

The girl turned to look in the direction of the detective and shook her head.

'I cannot leave my desk for long. As you can see, we are all very busy. I will ring you in an hour when my shift finishes at six. That's the best that I can do.'
Heather raised her eyebrows at the audacity of the woman and watched as she stamped her way back to her desk. She had half a mind to sit and wait for her, but was worried about catching something from the old guy who was continuously coughing and snorting the back of his throat.

They sat outside watching the surgery and waited for her to leave the building. 6.15 came and the young receptionist locked the door and pulled the steel shutters down.

'Excuse me.' Heather shouted from the car window. 'Is Kate Thomas still there?'

The receptionist walked over to the car, holding her bag over her arm while foraging for her car keys.

'No, she's already left. We leave through the back door. Some of these patients don't understand the pressure we receptionists are under, so we try to avoid any confrontation.'

Heather wound the window up and got Woods to ring the station to find out her home address. After turning the corner to enter her street, they encountered an irate man outside the house, banging the windows and shouting erratically. 'You thieving bitch! You won't hear the end of this.' As Woods got out of the car, the man shouted back at him.

'Don't do any work for her, mate. She won't pay you.'

He slammed his carpenter's van door shut, revved his engine and drove off, leaving the woman fuming on the doorstep.

'Did you see that? Call yourselves police officers. You could see he was clearly out of control.'

'Miss Thomas, the man seemed very annoyed at you for not paying him for something. It's not our job to get involved in petty arguments. Can we come inside?' When they entered the house, the smell of new wood hit their nostrils. It was obvious by its state of near finish that the kitchen was being refurbished. The oak cabinets were immaculate, and you could tell that this had been the creation of a professional who was very proud of his work.

'Don't look at it. I'm not happy with it, and that's that.'

'It's not for us to get involved with Miss Thomas. Now, as I said earlier, we need to know more about the days before your father's passing. Did you visit him? Or did he have any other visitors?'

She looked at them with a face like a soured lemon. 'Who would want to visit him? He was half dead before he went in there. He has no friends, well, none that would be up to visit him.' She made it obvious that she wanted the conversation to end, as she hadn't welcomed them into the living room to sit down. 'I saw him on Friday, and he died on Monday. That was it.'

There were no tears. Her face was just as hard as it was before. Normally at times like this, recalling someone's death would bring a show of emotion, or at least some reaction to what was being said, but there was nothing. They could have been talking about the death of a complete stranger.

'I've never trusted that home. They were always ringing me, reminding me to visit, then getting in a huff when I couldn't give them a date for their diary. I found it very rude. And very suspicious. How dare they insist that I visit him!'

'I'm sure they were only doing what was best for your father, Miss Thomas.'

The woman sucked through her teeth at their humbling comment. 'If they were doing their best, they wouldn't have let him be robbed by his carers, Detective. The matter is still ongoing, and I haven't heard a thing back from the station regarding it.'

'Miss Thomas, I can assure you we are aware of the withdrawals and are looking into each case separately. Do you know of any names that your father may have mentioned?'

'As I said detective I'm a very busy woman, so I hadn't seen my father since last year. I have access to his account so when I noticed money was missing I informed the home and you lot.' She shook her head 'Don't know why I bothered though as nothing has been done.'

She pushed her way past the standing detectives and opened the front door.

'We are not finished yet, Miss Thomas. I'm having trouble understanding why in all the time that we have been here you haven't displayed any emotion over your father's death'.

'Well, that's another thing you don't seem to have investigated very well. First, they tell me that he died in his sleep and now they've suggested that he may have been murdered. Which is it?'

She held onto the door, adamant not to shut it and offer any welcome.

Heather looked at the open door and then back at Kate.

'If you would rather come down to the station, Miss Thomas, we can do this there. But we do need to investigate this. Shall we start with your whereabouts over the last two weeks?'

The woman huffed and scowled her face up even more. 'If you think that I have had anything to do with his death, you are sorely mistaken. I hated the man, yes. But he was my father. And I'm not enjoying your insinuations.'

'Is there anyone else that would benefit financially from your father's death, Miss Thomas?'

'No. Apparently, there is an illegitimate son somewhere, but as no one seems to know his name or whereabouts, it appears that I am still his only heir. I'm not even sure if he actually exists.

Heather began to feel a little sympathy for the woman. It appeared that she had not had a good relationship with her father. She shut down her notebook and made her way towards the door.

'OK, Miss Thomas, we will leave it here for today. I will need to speak to you again soon though, when the time is more convenient for you.'

She nodded her goodbyes and gently nudged Shane through the open door. As they walked down the path, Heather was aware that the woman was still watching them, as if to make sure that they leave.

'Not the loving daughter type, then?'

Heather shook her head at him and started the engine.

'We had a call from the station when you were in there. Mrs Rees has given us the names of the carers. There were four. Three of them are still at the home, the other Sue Evans left the day before he died.'

'That's interesting. Make her our first contact. Also, see if you can arrange a time at the home for Josh Bennet to get down there and interview the other three. I don't want to rule anyone out just yet.'

Chapter Three

The address that Sunnyville had given them for Sue Evans turned out to be a disused lock-up. They had looked around the surrounding areas, but the place was in too much disarray to have ever been lived in.

She sent Shane back to the office to do some more digging. With a name as common as Sue Evans in Wales, this was going to take some time. Heather decided to give the residential home another shot. There must be someone there with enough of a memory to tell whether they were being robbed, she thought.

This time Helen Rees showed her into the manager's office. It was evidently the best room in the building. The soft furnishings were expensive and there were no signs of any patient interaction in there. She acknowledged the manager's jumpy manner again and hoped that it was just a fear of relative retaliation and not something more sinister that was causing her state of unrest. She would hate to think of these old dears in any danger.

'As I said on the phone, Sue had only worked here for a couple of months and had left with no explanation. She just stopped coming in. We had tried to contact her countless times, but the mobile number we had for her is now void. She was also owed a week's back-pay but the account that they usually paid her wages into had also ceased.'

'How strange. Can I ask how she got the job here? Did she provide any references? Or past employment?'

'Well, yes, I'm assuming she did. The head office would be able to help you out with that more than I. We are a branch of a much bigger company. I'll give you their number.'

Heather took the opportunity to take a look around the residential home again. She walked into the garden and admired the fresh flowers that had bloomed. Under the canopy, she saw a familiar face. She bent down beside the woman so as not to startle her. At first, the woman's gaze seemed to look right through her, but then a spark of recognition filled her tired old face. Heather smiled and took her hand.

'Sheila Taylor. Oh, my goodness. I'd heard that you'd been released.'

The woman just carried on smiling. Heather pulled up a chair next to her, hoping that the woman wouldn't mind if she joined her.

'It's a lovely day, Sheila. These flowers are beautiful, don't you think?' After a few moments of silence, and no reply, Heather was about to leave her in peace.

'Yes, they are. Especially the heather over there by the stand.' The woman laughed. 'I bet you thought I was like these old dodders in here without a voice.' She pulled her blanket across her knees.

'I would never have thought that Sheila, you found your voice a good while back and surprised us all.'

The woman felt proud that she had remembered.

'That I did, my darling, that I did.'

As they both sat admiring the flowers, Heather heard a familiar voice and then footsteps coming towards them. She was carrying a small holdall with clothes and shoes that were threatening to fall out of it.

'There you are Mam, I've been looking all over for you.' As Jamie got close, Heather's stomach flipped just like it always did when she was around. Whilst pulling up a chair, she mistook Heather for a carer and apologised to her without looking at her directly.

'I'm sorry I'm late. I got stuck in traffic.'

As Heather raised her head, she greeted her with a smile before the biggest hug that nearly knocked her off her chair.

'Oh my god Heather, it's so good to see you.'

Sheila watched as the two women embraced. The chemistry between them was still as apparent as when they were sixteen and newly in love. Holding each other as if time had stood still, and they were back in school waiting for class to end.

As Heather sat back down, Sheila grabbed her arm. She had a feeling that she knew the new visitor that had joined them but couldn't place her exactly. She leaned into Heather so as not to embarrass herself.

'Is she a relative of Jimmy's? If she is, you can tell her right now that he still hasn't come to see me. He promised me that he would take me dancing the next time he was home on leave.'

Jamie smiled at her mother whilst swallowing down the lump that was swelling in her throat.

'It's me Mam, Jamie.'

The woman stared at her in confusion and then smiled. 'Of course, it is my darling girl. Tell this lovely lady to go and get us some tea.'

Heather could feel Jamie's pain. She had had an aunt with dementia, and she knew just how cruel her words could be. She looked over at Jamie. The woman looked lost as if she didn't know how to respond.

'How long has she been like this?'

Jamie shrugged her shoulders. 'I'm not really sure. When she went into prison, she just started forgetting things. At first, I thought it was just the shock of the trial and getting banged up for two years. As you know, thanks to you, she was getting on with rebuilding her life and was starting to live again. But that bloody trial took ages to come to court, and we all thought that the judge would have said that she had suffered enough. So many people off the estate had come forward to say that she had lived a life of hell with him.'

'It shocked us all, Jamie. The judge explained to us after the trial that as it was not strictly in self-defence that she killed your father, she would have to have some sort of custodial sentence. I suppose she was lucky that it was only two years. I'm sorry I didn't stay in touch. I had this nasty case that I was involved in and it took up a lot of my time.' Heather wished that she had made more of an effort, but as always, work had got in the way.

She was allowed to make time for her in the beginning, as she had been working on the case. Jamie and Sheila had been really grateful. It was when they passed the sentence that Heather found it hard to still be a friend to Sheila and keep her distance as a police officer. Her chief had told her not to get too close and to keep things on a more professional level. She was regretting this now.

'I did visit your mam a couple of times whenever I was down there with work. Did she say?'

Jamie just shook her head. She had been so glad to see Heather, but her mother being away with the fairies always unsettled her, especially when she mentioned her dead father, Jimmy. The name still brought the fear of God into her every time she thought of him.

Her mother had killed him in self-defence as she would not have survived another attack from him. But now, she couldn't remember any of it. The beatings and the violence he dished out to Sheila, Jamie and her brother Michael had been forgotten. Sometimes Jamie saw it as a blessing. Before her mother had admitted that she had killed him, it had seemed like she had shocked herself into believing it hadn't happened. Either that or Alzheimers was beginning to set in. As long as she believed that it hadn't happened, the longer it remained a dream. The admittance had made her realise that she had lost her last hope of him ever coming back. Although the man was a monster, she had always blamed herself and hoped that Jimmy would change his ways.

Her guilt from her one-night stand with her neighbour Tom, many moons ago, had had her locked in a violent marriage for years. It had given her another child, Michael, but Jimmy knew that the boy wasn't his from the moment he was born. He hated him.

Now, she had done her time and paid for her crime. But although she was physically free from him, he was still alive in her memory. But only as the young Jimmy. The one that loved her more than the moon and stars, as he would tell her whenever he came home on leave from the army. Jamie hoped and prayed to God that when she regressed, the memory would always have him being that age. That way, there would be no fear in her confused heart, just distant memories that felt like they had happened yesterday.

Heather left to get them some tea and when she arrived back, it was as if a light had turned back on in Sheila's mind. She recognised Heather straight away; it was as if the time-lapse had never happened.

'Heather, how lovely to see you!' She turned to Jamie 'This is the one you shouldn't have let get away.' Jamie, shocked by her mother's comment, jumped in to save face. 'Mam, you can't say that. You're embarrassing the poor woman.'

Heather was grateful for the interruption. 'How is life treating you, Jamie Sullivan?'

She shrugged her shoulders. 'Manic, as ever. It's a bit easier now they are both in school, though.'

'I can only imagine.' Heather had put the thoughts of starting a family well into the back of her mind. Her job was her baby. 'I had no idea that your mam had been released, or I would have made it over to visit. Did she come straight here?'

'Sadly yes. She hasn't got any memories of her time with Tom, so it wouldn't have been fair on either of them for Mam to go back and live with him on the estate.'

Jamie broke the silence that followed. 'So, are you here because of that money going missing and the old geezer popping his clogs?'

'Now you know, Miss Sullivan, I can't talk to you about police work, but yes.'

The two were getting acquainted, just like old times. They hadn't noticed that Sheila had started crying. When the sobbing became audible, Heather held her hand and stroked it gently. The woman looked back at her and copied the stroking with her other hand. 'When is my Jimmy coming to see me?'

The moment was unbearable. They didn't want to tell her the truth, but they didn't want to lie to her either. Just then, a carer came to their rescue.

'Hey Sheila, I think it's about time we got you in for some food, my love. Say goodbye to the ladies.'

Sheila waved, and as Jamie went in to kiss her mother, she pushed her away. This was the worst thing about the horrible illness. No one could prepare you for the rejection from the one you love, she thought. You know that it's not their fault, but it hurts like hell all the same.

Heather held Jamie in her arms. At that moment, they both shared the feeling of hardship for Sheila. For all these years, her life had been taken away from her by Jimmy, and now, when she was finally free, it was slowly being taken by another kind of monster.

Jamie released herself from Heather's hold and dried her eyes. 'I'm OK, I'm OK, it just gets to me sometimes.' Heather understood the need to try to regain decorum.

'Look, why don't we go for food? You can tell me all about Sarah and those beautiful kids.'

As soon as she mentioned the kids, Jamie looked at her watch. 'Oh, no, is that the time? I have to pick Molly up from gym practice. I'll definitely do a rain check, though.'

Heather looked a bit put out that her old friend was brushing her off.

'Honestly, I do have to go, this being a parent, lark takes up all of your spare time. Maybe you and Gareth could come over for a meal sometime?'

Heather had yet to tell Jamie the details of her and her ex-husbands parting ways, and today wasn't the right time. When she left Gareth to live her life with Martha, it was by mutual agreement between friends, as Gareth had also wanted to spend his life with someone else. It would take more than a matter of minutes to explain to someone that had not known the full details of their open marriage arrangement. If their paths were to cross again, she would try to explain. Heather simply air-kissed Jamie as she left, hoping this would be sooner rather than later.

On the way back, she was debating whether she would tell Martha later that she had bumped into Jamie.

The feeling of seeing her again had felt special, and she didn't want Martha to burst her bubble just yet. There was no way that Jamie would want anything to do with her now anyway, she thought. She had the beautiful caring Sarah. She was softer than wool and gave Jamie the loving security of a family. Something that Jamie had never had. She had turned out to be a good parent, too. That was obvious by her reaction to not turning up late to pick up her daughter. No, she would put all romantic thoughts about Jamie back in the bottom of her heart where they had been since their first kiss at sixteen.

By the time she got back to the station, the photocopies of Sue Evans's passport and other documents were already on her desk. They had been faxed straight through by Sunnyville's head office. Heather was pleased with the prompt response.

The copy of the passport was a little blurred, but she could make out the address as being on the Beechwood estate. At least she knew that this wasn't a disused warehouse.

Shane had joined her with two lukewarm cups of station coffee. Neither of them would enjoy the slosh, but it was something to keep their thirst at bay.

'So, we have a passport here with an address for the Beechwood Estate. This is where we need to start looking, Shane.'

Shane rolled his eyes. He hated the estate due to the number of police officers that had spent time in the Gwent hospital after having bricks thrown at their heads.

'Do I have to come? Can't you take someone... bigger?'

Heather laughed. 'It's not all bad down there, Shane. It's not as if they are burning cars on every corner. There are a lot of good people. It's only got a bad reputation from the new wannabe gangsters that have taken to patrolling the streets. You're a big enough boy, you can handle yourself against a few kids. By the way, this address is on the left side, so not so bad. Grab your coat.'

The estate had hardly changed since Heather was young. There had been minimal improvements made by the council, but they had managed to cage the old shopping centre in. It was like a scene from Colditz down there. They had replaced the graffiti that she had been used to seeing with new names and threatening slogans. But the smell was still the same. As they came over the hill, there was an upside-down car smouldering at the entrance of the lane. Three kids on bikes were shouting abuse at the firemen who were packing the gear back into the van. Shane looked over at Heather and gave her a smug smile of *I told you so*.

They found the address and were surprised to find that it was a modest semi-detached. The gardens were neatly kept, and there was a nice car in the driveway. She didn't know what to expect, but after talking to a few of the other carers about Sue, the impression had been of a single woman. And of someone who seemed to move from place to place with a mouth like a docker.

After noticing the child's bike in the driveway, she went back to check the address twice. The other care workers had also said that Sue had lived alone and had no children.

Dai Evans, Sue's husband, answered the door. His son Jake squeezed past to get out and jumped on the bike that was laying there. He apologised for the boy's intrusion as he tried to work out who his visitors were.

'Hello, I'm DI Williams and this is DI Woods. Is it OK if we step inside for a moment?'

Dai nodded, and the boy rode off on his bike. As they entered, they noticed large boxes in the living room, waiting to be unpacked.

'Sorry about the mess. We have a new TV entertainment system to put together and it's taking me some time.'

Shane looked at the expensive make on the side of the box and felt a twinge of jealousy. 'Wow, that must have cost a pretty penny.'

'It did. My wife treated me to it.'

The officers looked at each other with a copper's nod. Shane continued, 'Bit of a money bags your wife, is she?'

Dai shook his head. 'Nah, I wish. A patient that had passed away left her some money. The old lady didn't have any relatives apparently, so left Sue some money in her will, sad really.'

Heather looked around. The house was reasonably tidy and had no signs of any domestic trouble.

'Is your wife here, Mr Evans? We need to ask her some questions.'

'You've just missed her. She has left to care for a patient.'

They looked at each other again. Things were falling into place, it seemed.

'So is she still working as a carer?'

'Yes, that's all she knows.' Dai was starting to feel a little uncomfortable. 'Look, is there a problem I can help you with?'

'No, like I said, I need to ask her some questions about the time she worked for Sunnyville residential Home.'

Dai Evans looked confused. He had never heard of the place.

'Christ, she hasn't been moonlighting again, has she?'

The officer kept silent, waiting for the man to finish.

'Moonlighting, you know, doing another job when you are holding down a permanent position.' The man looked agitated at their vacant expressions. 'A year ago, I found out that she was working in a pub for extra cash. She didn't tell me about it. I only found out when one of the boys at work told me that they had seen her there. Is that it? Are you working for the taxman or something?'

At that moment, Heather had a message on her radio to contact the station. Shane kept the husband talking about what kind of equipment he was about to install, and he was showing Shane inside the box when Heather came back into the room.

'We are off now, Mr Evans, but before we go, do you think that you could write down your wife's work address for me? That would be a great help. '

He handed her the address scrawled on the back of a packet of Rizla, and they left.

Heather had received news from the station. A police check had been made on the address, and it had flagged up that Sue Evans had been arrested a few years back for bodily harm. The victim dropped the charges, but he needed to be hospitalised.

'We need to find this woman and bring her in. There are so many coincidences here, don't you think? New expensive gifts, form for violence.'

Shane added his knowledge to the list. 'I looked at that stuff and I don't think that it was bought honestly either. The instructions had one of those numbers on it, you know, the ones like at the police auctions. Looks like his wife is a bit of a liar as well.'

They turned up at the address that the husband had given. It was a private house in Langstone. An old man in his 70s answered, and he was visibly shaking.'

'She's gone. I tried my best to wake her up, but she's dead.'

They started checking the rooms of the house, and Heather found a lady unresponsive slouched on the settee. She called out to Shane, who was checking the rooms upstairs.

'I've found her.' Shane came running down the stairs two at a time.

'You had better call an ambulance, Shane. I can feel a weak pulse, but I don't like her chances. While you're at it, put out an APB for Sue Evans. This is more than a coincidence now.'

## Chapter Four

'What the fuck!'

Ruby crumpled up the note that her mum had left for her. She was hoping to come home to a nice cooked tea after the day she had had. But no. She had packed her brother off to his nans to sleep over, and then she was off down the bingo again.

She hated coming home to an empty house. The estate was always alive with lowlifes at this time of night. She could smell the weed in the air from next door already. She only had to sit in her garden for ten minutes and she would feel some effect from it.

Last week, she watched as a black BMW pulled up and two blokes came out wielding machetes. They booted the door in, but luckily for the neighbour he had already been arrested and was down the nick. She hated having to move back to her old place, but after her brother Jack's death, there had been no other choice.

As she walked from the kitchen, the phone rang. It startled her and she made her way back through with a frown. 'Hello.... Hello.' She could hear breathing on the other end, so was apprehensive about ending the call. 'Who's there? Who is it?'

Eventually, she put the phone down, and it rang again. No-one was there. 'Look, I know someone is there as it sounds like Darth fucking Vader with all that breathing.' She slammed the phone down and nearly made it to the living room before it rang again. This time she screamed down the phone 'For fuck's sake.'

'That's no way to talk to your mother.'

'Sorry Mum. Why didn't you answer me? — Never mind. Whats up?'

'I'm just ringing to tell you that I will be late home tonight. Your little brother is at his nan's, so you'll have to cook your own tea.'

'You left me a note, remember? I thought it was me with the memory loss, not you, but thanks for telling me... twice.'

Her mother stayed silent for a few brief seconds. She knew that she had left her a note, but with her problems, she wanted to make sure she had read it properly. Since the accident, she hadn't been herself. She was a lot more placid and laid back. She had secretly hoped that the new Ruby would stay, the old one was much too volatile and had got herself mixed up in things that only a mother would forgive her for.

'Now listen Ruby. You take it easy now and stay inside. I don't want you walking around the estate on your own. You know what it's like out there.'

She knew only too well what the Beechwood estate was like. Since she came out of the hospital, her memory was starting to come back. She could remember a lot of things that she didn't want to, especially about her brother.

In her memory, it was him that pushed her over the edge of the cliff and left her for dead, but she didn't know why. She couldn't remember getting to the spot at the edge of the welsh mountain, but she could see his face as she fell. She would wake up in the middle of the night from feeling her brother's hands clasped around her neck. And then nothing. The sense of falling always woke her.

She still loved him. And missed him every day. How could it have been him that had put her into that coma? He was her protector. She had never told a soul about him pushing her. The police had told her that there was an eyewitness that had seen them arguing, but she hadn't confirmed it to them. If she still had doubts, she wasn't going to let the memories of her dead brother be tainted in that way. Some days, she wished she could remember more about the months leading up to her accident, but other days she knew that they would only haunt her. Her doctors had told her to stay away from any police questioning, as the subject could cause a relapse. There was cast iron proof that her brother had killed Frankie though, as the police had had ringside seats when he pulled the trigger. But they couldn't bring him to justice as straight after that, he had put the gun to his head and ended all his sadness.

She put the kettle on and filled her mug with milk and sugar before running upstairs to get changed. When she came down, there was another cup next to hers filled with milk and sugar. She called out to see if her mother had changed her mind and come home early. Then realised that she would have never made that drive in the time it took her to get dressed. She took a quick scan around the house, but nothing. She must be going crazy, she thought.

As she moved into the living room, she could see that the front window was wide open. She hadn't noticed it when she first came in, so started to feel anxious. She walked back into the kitchen, along the hallway, and up the stairs. Her previously broken limbs still gave her problems when standing too long, but she had never allowed herself to be the victim. She called out again and waited for a response, but nothing.

She walked into her bedroom, and there on the bed was a note. *Come and find me.*

That was the last thing she wanted to do, but going outside would be worse. She had no people close enough to her to offer any security, so no one to knock for help. She would have to deal with this herself. She picked up her bedside lamp with the heavy brass bottom and gingerly walked back down the stairs. The living room light was now on and Frankie's daughter Chloe, who had been Ruby's childhood friend, was sitting on the settee, coffee in hand.

'So, this is nice after all these years.' She looked down at the lamp in her hand. 'You won't need that. I put the light on for you.'

A startled Ruby strained her eyes to focus on the figure sitting in her living room.

'What the fuck? Did you break in here? You don't scare me, you know. I've been to hell and back and got the fucking t-shirt.'

'Chill, Ruby it's me.'

Ruby moved in closer, and her eyes adjusted to the light. She wasn't expecting to see a familiar face from her childhood. The woman had changed a lot. But she could still recognise that beautiful red hair.

'Chloe? Is that you?'

The woman just smiled. Then her smile turned to a deadly stare. 'I thought you'd be pleased to see me.'

Ruby was dazed. 'What are you doing in my house?'

'I'm back for my old man's money, ain't I.' She patted the seat next to her to instruct Ruby to join her. 'Sit down then. I'm not straining my neck to look up at you.'

Ruby declined and sat on the seat opposite.

Chloe took a sip of her coffee and screwed her face up before placing the cup on the table. 'That's that cheap coffee from down the shops, ain't it? I'd know that taste anywhere. It's fucking horrible.' She lifted her legs onto the settee to get comfy. They stared at each other for a short while, and then, after reading Ruby's face, she spoke.

'I miss him too, you know.'

Ruby looked at her, then narrowed her eyes. 'Who? Frankie? He was a total bastard. How can you possibly miss him?'

Chloe raised her head in disbelief. 'No, not fucking Frankie, Jack. I'm just saying that I miss him, too.'

She paused for a while in thought. Ruby found it strange to hear someone else mention his name. It had been ages since anyone had dared to. Even though he had killed the most hated man on the estate, the local gossip still classed him as a murderer.

'The best thing he ever did was kill my old man. Did he tell you that he came to see me the day he died?'

Ruby shook her head in disbelief. It had been almost a year since his death. With her memory still not firing on all cylinders, she wouldn't have remembered if he had told her or not.

'Yup, he turned up at my works, firing questions at me about that fucking diary that you stole from me.'

'What? How did he know where to find you?'

'Ah, me and Jack went way back. I can't believe he never told you. We had this—thing going on. He would call me up and we'd spend the night together. Nothing serious, just good friends. Then I heard through the gossip that he had got involved with my old man. I couldn't stand him after that. He kept telling me that it made no difference. But he didn't know what that bastard was capable of, not like us.'

Ruby didn't know how to react, but attempted to engage. 'Sorry, I didn't know.'

'Why should you? He never knew anything about me. I don't let anyone know anything about me.'

She went to pick up the coffee cup again, then thought better of it.

'So why are you here? In my house now? Surely, you're not after an apology for stealing that diary.'

The woman laughed. 'No, nothing like that. Jack told me that you had become something of a wildcard, so I thought I'd come and see for myself, being as I'm back on our beloved estate.'

Ruby stood up and looked out of the window across the green. 'Yup, it hasn't changed. Still the same shit hole we are all drawn back to.'

Chloe agreed. 'Ah, the Beechwood estate. The place where everyone wants to move away from then ends up coming back to die.'

Ruby didn't want to believe that Jack had had anything to do with Chloe. She didn't even know if he had told her about them. If he did, surely this is something she would have remembered. After all, they were childhood friends and Jack didn't know anything about the abuse they both suffered at the hands of Frankie Thompson. Their lives changed the day that the bastard drugged his daughter and her friend. They hadn't even reached ten. This moulded the two. From then on, neither girl could trust anyone in their life. They had both lived in their own private turmoil.

'So, has anyone heard anything from my brothers? I'm not expecting Wayne to turn up for the reading of the will as I think he's still inside, but Kevin may have the balls, to. That's if he's still got any balls. Did you know he's a shirt lifter now?'

Ruby knew. So did the rest of the estate. Frankie's gay son. He had been banished from the family home. Never to be seen or heard from again.

'So you think you got a chance to get your hands on all that dirty money and thought you'd come here to gloat, is it? Now that my family are back, stuck on the Beechwood estate.'

'Well, yeah, sort of.' Chloe pointed her finger at Ruby's face. 'You fucking left me. I know that we were only kids, but when you moved off the estate, you didn't want anything to do with me. I even came looking for you a couple of years later. You knew it was me at your door. Do you know how much fucking guts it took for me to do that? To just turn up like that. I suppose it was easy to just forget me when you had your new daddy Phil to look after you all.'

Ruby knew she was right. She had thought of contacting Chloe but didn't want to be around the one person that knew her secrets. The plan was to start again. Bury the dark memories of Frankie and her own father's death and make new ones.

'I waited for ages for you to at least send me a letter to say that you missed me, but nothing. We were like sisters, linked in arms against the wrath of Frankie and nothing. Some fucking friend you were. Especially as I was keeping your secrets.'

The girls had practically lived in each other's houses growing up. Both of them had hated their fathers for one reason or another. They had become allies in a dangerous world. When Ruby's father died at her own hands, nobody had known about it, except for Chloe. Chloe could have dropped her friend deep in the shit by opening her mouth, but she never did.

'Ah, right, so that's it. After all these years, you're gonna open your mouth about that. You were no innocent Chloe. You kept a lookout when I put those tablets in his beer. If I get done for it, I'll take you with me.'

'I don't know what you're talking about, Ruby. I heard on the news that Jack had killed both your dad and your stepdad Phil. He confessed, didn't he? Before he shot his fucking brains out.'

'Yes, and that's how it is going to stay. Jack can't get hurt anymore in this, but my mother can.'

Chloe gazed over at the family photo that was sitting above the TV. She remembered when the photo was taken over by the quarry. She wanted to sit in on it, but Ruby wouldn't let her. She said it was for family only.

'How is your mam, Ruby? Is she still getting pissed every night down the bingo?'

'Nah teetotal now since we moved off the estate.'

Chloe smiled. 'That won't last long now that she's back. I always liked your mam. She was kind, and I always thought that you were so lucky. My mother envied her, you know. I think she had a bit of a thing for your dad. Before he died, she was always saying he was a nice bloke, but then again, she had to put up with Frankie. Hitler was a nice bloke compared to him.'

Both girls laughed.

'She liked you too, Chloe. She hated hearing the shouting and fists flying at your mother from Frankie. She used to tell my dad to go and help but he never did. None of his business, he used to say.' It was the way things were done on the estate. Frankie had never come nosing when he was having a barney with his family, either. Everything was private behind your own front door.

Frankie made her flesh crawl. Every time they had a street party, he would squeeze past her, placing his hot, sweaty hands around her waist.

Chloe sighed, then smiled. 'Well, he got what he deserved in the end. I wish that I had been there to see him bleed out. I would have planted one last kick on his sorry arse.'

Both girls laughed again. Then silence shone through their memories of their distorted childhood.

'Ruby, do you think that you would have killed your dad if my dad hadn't fucked up your childhood? I mean, do you think that you were born a killer?'

Ruby didn't want to reply, as she would have had to come to terms with the answer. Yes, she killed her father and later did the same to her stepfather. But she had never been accused of it. Jack had confessed to both murders to protect his little sister, and the police had closed the case. But that detective Martha knew what she was capable of. With no proof, she would sit pretty in her own ignorance and hope to God that Chloe wasn't here to confess any sins.

'I'm just wondering if the chance came up, say for the money, or a ticket out of this place, would you do it again?'

If she was being honest with herself, she could answer straight away with a firm yes, but she didn't want to fall into any web that Chloe was weaving.

'I'm not going to knock your brother off for you, Chloe. Frankie wouldn't have had that much money left in his estate. The police would have taken most of it back as it was counterfeit.'

'No, I'm not suggesting that. I'm talking about strangers. With sheds load of cash that nobody knew about—and yeah, my stepfather Brian.'

Chloe could see her old friend Ruby's brain ticking away in that murderous head of hers. Even if she was portraying herself as a goody two shoes now. She couldn't fool Chloe.

'Who the fuck is Brian? And what has that poor bastard done to you?'

Chloe grimaced. 'Brian fucking Stanley is a controlling arsehole who has power over my life. Including my finances. If, and it's a big if, I get any money from Frankie's will, I won't see a penny of it if Brian is still alive.'

She sat on the floor in front of Ruby. 'Frankie owes us that money. He took away our childhood and turned us both into monsters. That money belongs to us. Just think. You could move off the estate and never worry about work again. Your brother could go to a better school and wouldn't get picked on by the bullying bastards at Beechwood High. You've done this before, Ruby, twice. I'm sure once more wouldn't hurt.'

'Once more would fucking hurt if I get caught, though.'

Chloe smiled at Ruby. 'I fucking knew it. You didn't correct me. You killed Phil as well, didn't you? Jack was covering your arse for both murders.'

Ruby stayed silent. She didn't want to dig herself into that hole any deeper.

'Look, Ruby, all I'm saying is, if you help me get rid of fucking Brian, we can both start again. It's not like anyone will come after us. He's just a sad fucking bank manager with a golf obsession that's nearly as big as his arse.'

'Why don't you just pay someone to rob the bank?'

'I knew you were on the same wavelength as me. That is exactly what I thought. Pay someone to rob the bank and get him shot during the raid. Then it would look like it was about the money and not him personally. Do you think you could handle a gun?'

Ruby cocked her eyes. 'I didn't mean me, you daft twat. I meant someone from Frankie's gang. There is bound to be someone around that would do it for a couple of grand.'

They both discussed it for a while, then decided it would be too dodgy. Most of Frankie's loyal men had gone down with him. The only ones that were left would probably double-cross them in a blink of an eye.

'It has to be just you and me, Ruby. We are the only ones that should gain from Frankie's money. At least think about it, yeah. Now, what have you got planned for tea? I'm starving.'

## Chapter Five

Martha came back from the bar with drinks in hand. She had been admiring the restaurant's decor on the way through. She put down the glasses and pointed to the feature wall.

'That's the colour I was thinking of painting the living room.'

It was dark green and had framed photos of various types of pasta arranged in an arch. Heather wasn't so sure. At first, she bit her lip before responding, but then couldn't help herself. The woman had no taste. 'Don't you think that would be a little dark? The place needs lightening up, to show off the sea view. I could always help with the interior design of the place if you'd like me to?'

Martha tutted. 'No. My house, my choice. I like it with a warmer feel.'

This was typical of Martha. Heather had been spending a lot of time there. She had thought that by doing things like the supermarket shop together and sharing some of the bills she may begin to think of it as their place. But as Martha had insisted on being in charge of everything, she had no way of knowing what direction the relationship was going in. Or whether moving in together would ever happen.

The vibration of Heather's phone was a welcome disturbance. She frantically moved things around in her bag to find it. When she finally answered the call, she was excited to hear the news.

'Good work Shane. But don't talk to her until I get there, OK.' Heather had been waiting for this. 'Martha, I'm sorry I'm going to have to leave you with the bill for lunch, I'm afraid. They've just found Sue Evans.'

'For fuck's sake Heather, every time.' Martha pushed her plate of spaghetti carbonara away from her.

'You know the score Martha, you were a copper for long enough.'

She did know the score, but she was used to being the one that disappeared on dates, not the one left hanging.

'I'll come with you. Just let me get the bill.'

Heather already had her coat on and her keys in her hand. 'No time, sorry love. I'll pop round and see you later, yeah?'

Heather didn't wait for an answer. She had to get to the station.

When she arrived, she observed the woman sitting in the interview room. She looked nothing like she had imagined. Through the glass, she saw a middle-aged woman in a carer's uniform. The look on her face was one of concern. But then her copper's mind kicked in. It's never the ones you think. They are the worst to convict.

After introducing herself and making her aware that the conversation was being recorded, She noticed that Sue was looking overly nervous. No one had explained to her why she was taken in and she was fearing the worst regarding her family.

'Can someone please tell me what is going on? Nothing has happened to Jake or Dai, has it?'

Heather reassured her that it was nothing to do with any members of her family and began the interview.

At first, it was just to clarify her name and date of birth.

'Thank you, Mrs Evans. I'm sorry that it has taken so long for you to be interviewed. Due to the delicate matter of this enquiry, I wanted to interview you myself.'

The woman stirred in her chair.

'I also need to get a clear picture of the situation. I hear that you have declined your right to have a lawyer present. Is that correct?'

'Well, yes—I haven't done anything so I just want to get this over as soon as I can.'

Heather continued. 'Mrs Evans, I understand that you are a care worker and I need to know a little more about your relationship with one of the gentlemen. A Mr Thomas.'

'Thank God for that. I was so worried that it was something to do with a family member.' Sue breathed a sigh of relief. 'Mr Thomas, yes. He's a lovely man. How is he keeping?'

Heather looked surprised at Sue's response. 'He's not keeping very well, Mrs Evans. He's dead!'

Sue held her hand to her mouth. 'Oh, my goodness no. That didn't take long. I thought he would have had a few months left at least.'

'Can I ask you where you are working now, Mrs Evans?'

Sue looked a little confused at the question. She assumed that they would have already known if they were talking about Mr Thomas. 'I'm still working for Carers are Us. I have been for the last ten years.'

'When we were at your house. Your husband told us that you had received money from a patient that you had been looking after. Was that patient on the books of Carers are Us.'

Sue rubbed her hands down the front of her uniform. They were beginning to sweat, and she had felt put out that they had gone to her home.

'Look, I didn't want to take the money in the first place, but the relatives insisted. Is that what this is about? Have they changed their mind or something?'

Heather had no answer to the question, so moved on.

'According to your co-workers. You spent quite a bit of time with Mr Thomas before he died. Did you find his behaviour unreasonable? We were told that he used to lash out at the carers sometimes.'

'Unreasonable, no, never. He was the perfect gentleman. Are we talking about the same Mr Thomas? It's quite a common name, you know. I can't count how many times I have had a Mr or Mrs Thomas.'

'I am talking about Mr Les Thomas, Mrs Evans,'

Sue thought, then shook her head. 'I can't remember a Les Thomas, sorry?'

Heather rifled through her paperwork to find a picture of Les Thomas. Then showed it to Sue. She picked it up and moved the photo further away from her to focus.

'No, sorry love. I don't know this man. Who told you that I knew him? Was it one of the agency staff? They can get mixed up sometimes.'

Heather took the photo from her and placed it back on the table.

'He was at the Sunnyville Residential home when you were working there. He...'

Sue looked more confused than ever and stopped Heather in mid-conversation. 'What? I just told you I work for Carers are Us. I've never worked for Sunnyville residential home.'

Heather took out the photocopy of the passport. 'This is you, yes?'

This time she got her glasses out of her bag. While Sue was looking at it, she also pulled out the job application and list of referees.'Is this your handwriting?' Sue nodded her head. 'Look, Sue, we know that you may have wanted it to be kept quiet from your husband for whatever reason, but you can't lie to the police. If you have never worked there, then how would we have all of this documentation from the head office?'

Sue was speechless. She couldn't defend herself, as she had no answers. She tried to explain that she had filled out an application form a while back to apply for the job but then stopped herself from saying any more. All she could say was that she didn't want to say anything else unless she had a lawyer.

Heather suspended the interview. Why had she changed her mind? She said that she hadn't done anything wrong. Something was up, she thought. A gentle knock at the door had Heather excusing herself to leave the room to answer a phone call. It was Shane. He had called in to say that the woman found at the address that Dai Evans had given them had died. Because of this, and not knowing the circumstances of the woman's death, they didn't want to risk releasing Sue back into the community. She may be a danger to the public. They would have to consider charging her for the suspicion of the murder of Les Thomas. A solicitor would now be assigned, and they would further their investigations.

\* \* \*

It was teatime at Sunnyville, and the place was a bustle of carers helping residents with their food. Today had been fish fingers, mash and peas with jam roly-poly and custard for pudding.

Heather noticed Sheila sitting in the corner, staring into space. She didn't want to startle her, so waved before she approached. The woman seemed to have a flicker of recognition, and Heather hoped that she would remember who she was.

'Hey Sheila, did you enjoy your tea?'

It was a good moment. Sheila remembered Heather and greeted her with a smile.

'The food is not very nice in here, Heather. It's like bloody prison food.' She laughed 'I should know.'

Heather was glad that she could joke about it. She was wrongly imprisoned but there had been nothing anyone could have done to stop it from happening.

'Why don't you ask Jamie out for food again when she comes in? I heard her turn you down last time.'

Her suggestion surprised Heather. 'Don't go getting any ideas now, Sheila. You know that she is spoken for.'

The woman looked at her 'She isn't you know.' Heather whispered, 'I wish' under her breath. She said her goodbyes and made her way to the office to look at the CCTV system that the home was using. This was the reason for her visit. There must be something, somewhere to catch out Sue, she thought.

Heather looked at the equipment. She didn't know a lot about technology, but this system looked like it belonged on the ark. There were a few CDs around the unit but not enough to form any system that may have been filed or documented.

'Do you have anything at all from the time that Sue was here?'

Helen Rees held up her hands. 'No, as I explained to your officers. The machine records over everything after a few months. It recycles itself.'

She urged the manager to take another look into any saved files. It was worth another try. Something may have been missed.

The tea-trolleys had taken over the corridors so Heather was escorted by Helen Rees through a different exit door, so as not to get in the way of the kitchen servers.

The place was a maze of glass fire doors and shiny floors. As they approached the back entrance, they had to wait for two college students and a tutor that were carrying boxes of pottery into the recreational room. Helen Rees explained that these would be used for the more able residents to paint for therapy and stroke rehabilitation purposes.

She took a quick look inside the room and noted the remnants of simple craft projects that were half-finished. Helen Rees explained further that the residents would sell them on open days and the carers would use the money to take the residents on days out to the park or the seaside.

Pinned to the notice boards were photographs of the residents at work. There were also a few showing various residents celebrating birthdays.

Heather smiled. 'They all look like they are having a good time.'

Helen smiled back. After taking another look at a particular photo, she pointed to a woman holding a birthday cake. 'That's Sue, there, to the left of the picture.'

Heather inspected the photograph. The face was covered, so unrecognisable but the body was clearly in the shot.

'Why doesn't this look like the Sue Evans I have down at the station?' She mumbled. The hair was a similar colour red, but the body frame was different. Her Sue was

much shorter and probably weighed at least three stones
heavier.

'Do you have any more photos?'

Helen shook her head. 'No, but there is a Facebook
page. She may be on a few of them.'

They went back into the office and the manager
loaded the page on her laptop. As they scanned through
the many, they found another two photographs. Each time,
she had chosen to cover her face. She was either very shy
in front of the camera or she wanted to hide her face for
anonymity. Heather was sure that it was a different person
and sensed a mistaken identity may have been had.

'Do you think you could pop down to the station
with me Mrs Rees? It won't take long. I think I need a
query cleared up.'

The woman managed to get herself relief cover at
the office and Heather drove her straight to the station in
her car. On the way, Heather couldn't resist chatting about
the late Mr Thomas. She was still concerned about the
reaction she had got when mentioning his wellbeing. After
seeing the photographs on the wall, she concluded that

Sunnyville was doing a sufficient job of looking after their residents.

'So, did Kate Thomas complain to you about the treatment her father was receiving at Sunnyville? It's just when we went to visit her, she seemed to be a bit concerned about her involvement with the home.'

'I'm sorry, Detective, if I'm speaking out of turn, but the woman is a very selfish individual. We try to encourage the family to visit if they are able. It is only a gentle phone call. Residents suffering from dementia may not recognise their relatives, but sometimes the familiarity of a face can stir some emotions. These people had a place in society. Some of them fought for their country. People sometimes forget that. We do not know if recognition does happen, but I believe that familiarity is the key to giving them some comfort out of life.'

Heather was quite surprised at the genuine concern coming from the woman. Some of the places that she had visited in the past had given her the impression that it was all about money. They would insist that cutbacks denied any chance of recreation for the residents. She was happy that this woman had the patient's well-being at heart.

At the station, Helen Rees waited for Sue to come into the viewing room. As she did, she immediately confirmed that this wasn't the Sue Evans that had worked at Sunnyville. There had been a terrible case of mistaken identity, and Heather wasn't sure how it had happened.

'Did you not notice at the time of the job interview that the passport's photo was not of the woman sitting in front of you, Mrs Rees?'

The woman looked confused and then redeemed herself. 'Well, no as I wouldn't have seen the actual passport. We don't deal with the identity checks at Sunnyville, we just interview the candidates. The head office gets sent the documents to check for references and such.'

This explained a lot of things. The Sue she interviewed didn't look like the type to have smothered someone with a pillow, and then spend time in a police interview room worried about her family. She arranged for Helen Rees to be driven back to Sunnyville and asked for Sue to be put into the interview room pending release.

The chief wasn't very happy at first. The mistake had cost the station a lot of time and effort, let alone the embarrassment of the ordeal. But after Heather had reminded him that this seemed a case of a stolen identity and that anyone would have come to the same conclusion, he let her off the hook.

Heather had a lot of explaining to do and gave Sue a heartfelt apology. Luckily for them, she was quite understanding about the situation. All she wanted to do was get home and forget about the whole thing.

When she arrived home, Dai wasn't as understanding. He had been at his wits' end worrying about his wife. He had imagined all sorts. Jake hadn't stopped crying that his mother wasn't coming home, and the neighbours had already come to their conclusions. The gossip hot line had her sentenced and convicted.

As Sue lay soaking in the bath, she put a damp flannel across her face. She had felt ashamed that she hadn't owned up to what may have happened. That list of referees that the detective had shown her was in her handwriting and she knew where and when the paper had gone missing. Could that woman have used her identity and taken the job that she was about to apply for? She assumed the place had been filled when she didn't hear back from Sunnyville, and never gave it a second thought.

Sue couldn't believe that this woman could be ruining her life again. There were so many lies that she had to tell to get her out of the mess. It had taken all of her strength to put things right.

Dai had never found out what had happened, and she had saved face. She had taken a part-time job and paid off the credit card in no time. He *had* found out that she was working at the pub, but she had made up the excuse of wanting to get him a special Christmas present and he had believed her. Sue had to cover that lie with another and bought the Christmas present from the catalogue.

When old Mrs Sims died, she paid the catalogue off outright. Sue had been caring for her over the last six months and had looked in on her even when it wasn't her shift. She was as surprised as anyone that the woman had left her a few thousand in her will. She had treated Dai to the entertainment system when one of the boys from the pub told her that his brother was selling them as knock-offs. She hoped to God that the police wouldn't be back at her house checking the serial numbers. She didn't think that they would though, as they had all been thankful that Sue hadn't kicked up a fuss at being falsely arrested. She couldn't kick up a fuss or the whole embarrassing story of how she gave three hundred pounds to a stranger would have come out then and there. Sue didn't want to be known as that vulnerable.

As the water washed away the stench of the police cell, she thought about the man that had been killed. Her conscience wouldn't allow her to keep quiet about the matter and wondered if she could tell the police what had happened without Dai finding out. She would sleep on it. Tomorrow she would be visiting the widower of her other patient. The poor love had died before Sue had had the chance to get to her. She had been called by another patient's family as their father had fallen off his commode. Life was never that easy.

She had told so many lies to cover up her stupidity, and she wished that she had come clean from the start. This time, there would be no option. She would have to tell the truth.

By the time Heather left the station, she didn't feel like going to Martha's. She had intended to, and got halfway up the M4, but was having trouble concentrating on the road. After battling with her conscience, she indicated her way off the slip road and went home to her little flat.

When she and Gareth split up, they sold the marital home and split the profit. She missed Gareth. Not in an ex-husband sort of way, but as a close friend. He always made her laugh, and she needed that sometimes. Being a police officer was always about the bad side of life, and she longed for laughter. All Martha wanted to talk about was police work, too. Her having to retire early through injury made her miss her beloved job. She loved it when Heather would come over and talk shop. It made her feel useful, and she missed the excitement of solving crimes. But all Heather wanted to do was talk about random things and shared memories. The only thing was that all the memories she had shared with Martha were at the station.

They had worked together at the same station for nearly fifteen years, so shared the same work past.

Watching Sheila and the rest of the people with Alzheimer's made her wonder where her life was going.

Even Jamie had settled into family life, which was something that she never thought she would see. She couldn't imagine Martha settling for something like that. She would have to give up putting herself first, so she knew that would never happen.

Before going to bed, she took out her old scrapbook from her school days. Her and Jamie's lives had both changed a lot since then. Sometimes she wished she could go back and do it all again. Then she remembered how much hassle they had from everyone and thought against it. To her, Jamie still looked exactly the same. Time hadn't aged her in the least. Heather wished that she could have thought the same about herself, but she had crow's feet appearing around her eyes and a few wrinkles to moisturise away each morning.

She poured the last of the bottle of wine she had been keeping for the weekend into her coffee cup. She hadn't been bothered to get herself a glass. She switched off the lights and took the book to bed. As she finally curled up under the duvet, she hoped that she would take the image of Jamie into her dreams. That way, she wouldn't have to feel guilty for the feelings that were stirring inside her.

Chapter Six

Helen Rees had found some more photos of their mysterious Sue Evans, so Heather stopped by to collect them. She still had an hour or two to kill before going back to the station, so she thought she would drop in on Sheila.

When she got to Sheila's side of the complex, she saw Jamie closing the door of her room. After the initial feeling of, *oh my god she's here* she called out to her.

'How's she doing?'

Jamie put her finger to her lip 'Sshh you noisy bugger. She's just fallen asleep in the chair.'

Heather laughed as they tiptoed away.

'Was your conversation that boring?'

Jamie wouldn't get her irony. She never did.

Jamie ran her hands through her hair. 'Probably. I never know what to say to her anymore. She was mainly off with the fairy's again today, talking about her old friend Sal. Apparently, she is going to ask her if she wants to go to the pictures on the weekend.'

'Aw, poor Sheila. Maybe you and Sarah could take her. They would probably let you take her out for a couple of hours.'

Jamie smiled and then narrowed her eyes. 'Look, have you got time for a coffee? We could go to the park opposite here. There's probably something I should tell you.'

Heather didn't need to be asked twice. They found a quiet bench under the trees and Jamie treated them to a couple of cappuccinos.

'Gareth wouldn't mind you being here with me, would he?'

Heather blew on her coffee and began to tell Jamie the complex story of her and Gareth's mutual parting.

She didn't quite know what to say about Martha. She told her that they were in a so-called relationship, but hadn't mentioned that every time she thought they were getting closer and would want to talk about their relationship, Martha would either change the subject or try to talk her out of making plans.

She noticed that Jamie looked like she was about to say something, but maybe couldn't find the words.

'It's OK. You can say it. *I told you so*. You knew that I would be back with a woman.'

Jamie let out a giggle but didn't claim I told you so. Heather then realised that she had held most of the conversation time as usual. She put her cup to one side and turned toward her old flame.

'Jamie, I'm so sorry. You were about to tell me something. You know what I'm like for rabbiting on.'

At first, Jamie shook her head as if she had changed her mind. But as Heather nudged her shoulder to spill the news, she turned away from Heather with her head bowed.

'Sarah's gone Heather. She died of cancer last year.'

There was silence between them both. Heather didn't know what to say and didn't want to ask overly obvious questions. She would just let Jamie tell her what had happened.

'Everything was going so well, you know. And then she started feeling run down and had this cough that she couldn't get rid of. She went for so many tests, but we had no idea. It was only a cough.' A single tear fell down Jamie's face, and she wiped it away with her sleeve.

'When the doctor gave us the news that it was cancer, it was already too late. It was at stage four, so they told us to prepare for the worst.'

Heather was now also holding back the tears. She had no idea. The last time she saw them both was when Sheila was sent down. She had meant to keep in touch, but that counterfeit case had taken her spare time away. She hated her job for always getting in the way of normal life. She went to put her arm around her old friend, but Jamie slid further down the bench.

'Sorry, Heather, but if you hug me, I won't be able to talk. I will be a blubbering mess.'

She understood. Caring contact did that to her, too.

'Silly question, I know, but how are the children?'

She wiped away both of her eyes and took a deep breath. 'They are doing OK, now. At first, Molly would call out for her all the time, then stop and remember that she wasn't home. Night time was the worst. In her dreams, she was still alive, and they were having fun together. So, when she awoke, she had to relive the feeling of loss all over again. It took her ages to readjust.' Jamie had to swallow her emotions whilst talking about how the kids had felt. 'Little Ricky, not so bad. He is only three, so was so young when it happened. I don't think he remembers her much. But then again, some days, I find him staring at her photo. So, who knows?'

'I think it's time for that hug now, Jamie.' She slid in closer and held her tight. As the tears streamed down both their faces, they sighed in sync and gave out a few laughs in their woeful state before Heather broke their silence.

'How about I treat us to an ice-cream in a bit when we are looking a bit more presentable? We can walk around this beautiful park and chat shit about anything.'

That was what Jamie needed. She hated having to explain to people, as it brought all the heartache back. When she was alone, she would sit and cry. But in public, she had to be strong for the kids. They had no chance of moving on if they saw their mother as a quivering wreck every day. So, she kept her tears just for herself. She would allow herself this brief outburst, then go back to remembering all the good times that she and Sarah had.

They had the most beautiful civil partnership service, with little Molly as a bridesmaid. Even Sheila had attended. Arm in arm with Tom. Times were so good then. Everyone looking forward to their future and not knowing anything about the terrible times that lay ahead.

As they walked through the park, Heather tried to change the mood. At first, the conversation was about the times that they had shared; nearly being caught doing things that they shouldn't have done as teenagers. Jamie told her about the time that she and Big Ricky had robbed an Ice-Cream van. They had nearly managed to drive it off the estate, but they couldn't turn the siren off, so were caught before they made it.

Before he died, Ricky had gotten her into so many dodgy situations it was a wonder that she ever became as respectable as she was now.

'Don't you ever repeat any of this to my kids? I want them to grow up on the right side of the law.'

Jamie's kids had already had a better start in life than she did. Apart from losing their other mother, of course. Jamie was bringing them up in a much more affluent place than the Beechwood estate. She would give them enough love from both of them and tell them every day how much she loved them. Sarah had made a few videos for their birthdays and other significant parts of their lives. She had wanted them to know that even though she wasn't physically there, she would always be watching over them, and Jamie. This had given them comfort, and they knew that it was the right thing to do. They were lucky that they had used the time they had left wisely.

'I won't tell them that you were once as infamous as Bonnie and Clyde if you don't tell them that I made the biggest mistake of my life, turning my back on you, and letting you deal with all that shit on your own.'

Jamie was a little shocked by Heather's comment. 'Maybe it's time that we let the past stay on the Beechwood estate.' Before any more painful memories crawled to the surface, she changed the subject by asking about the investigation. 'So, what about the trouble at Sunnyville? Are you any closer to knowing who stole the money? And who that poor guy's killer was?'

Heather knew that she really shouldn't talk about the case to Jamie, but as she had been visiting her mother there, she may know something that may help.

'Did you and Sheila know a carer there, called Sue Evans?' Jamie nodded. 'Yeah, I remember Sue. She had a mouth on her like a docker. A few of the old ladies used to take offence at her dropping the F-bomb all the time.'

Heather had heard that from a few others. 'Yeah, that's the one. What did you think of her, Jamie? Did your mam ever say anything about her?'

'Mam didn't mind her. Most of the time she probably confused her with someone else anyway. She does that sometimes. Have you noticed?'

Heather smiled. 'Yes. Sometimes I think that your mam recognises me then, at other times, I think she thinks that I'm a carer.'

Jamie knew how that felt. More often than not, Sheila greeted her as a distant relative of Jimmy's. She continued. 'She did say that listening to Sue was like listening to the neighbours on the estate. Well, I think that's what she was trying to say. She'd start to tell me something, then go off on a tangent about something else.

She didn't have that much to do with her personally. She worked a lot with the unruly male residents.'

Suddenly realising what she had said, Jamie came to her own conclusion. 'Wait, you don't think it was her, do you?'

Heather raised her eyebrows. She had probably said too much, but she knew that Jamie wouldn't repeat any of it. She had too much drama in her own life to worry about anyone else.

'She could be the type, you know. Stealing the card money, I mean. I don't think she would go as far as knocking them off.'

Heather was intrigued. 'Why do you say that?'

'Well, thieves are not always capable of murder, are they? They are just in it for the money. Pinching your wallet with a smile. She did take some stick off the blokes' mind. They were always grabbing at her. To be honest, I think she used to give them a quick kick under the wheelchair to stop it. Nah, I wouldn't think Sue was a murderer. Possibly a thief though'

Heather laughed at Jamie's way of thinking. You could take the girl off the estate, but you could never take the estate out of the girl. Still the same cheeky way of rationalising everything. Thieving from someone who was loaded would be forgiven. But you couldn't go as far as murdering them.

'Well, to be honest, we've just found out that Sue isn't who she is claiming to be. She is using someone else's identity. We haven't got a clue who she really is. Have you got anything that may help?'

Jamie paused for a brief moment. 'I did hear the girls calling her Red sometimes. Maybe it's a nickname. You could ask around if anyone knows the name Red. Try on the estate. You never know.'

Heather thought that Jamie may have had a point. She would ask her contacts on the estate. Anything was worth a try. The banks were refunding the stolen cash card money, so no one was out of pocket, but they needed a name for Red. If only to clear her of the crimes.

They walked back over to Sunnyville, as they had both left their cars there. The time that they had spent together had been good for them both.

After checking they had each other's current numbers and making promises to not lose contact again, they parted.

Jamie had to do the school run, and Heather needed to pay a visit to the real Sue Evans. She had called the station and asked if Heather would drop by and see her. Heather thought it was the least she could do after wrongly accusing her, but she hoped that she wasn't going to file a complaint. She wasn't in the mood for all that paperwork.

After remembering old memories with Jamie, driving through the Beechwood estate gave her a sense of belonging. For quite a while now, she had only visited the estate as a police officer. She had forgotten the times that she had spent there in her youth. The memories had all been entwined with crimes that she had witnessed.

When she pulled up in the car outside Sue's, she took a look at the scenery. The mountain, so visible in the distance, had always looked so beautiful. The trees and the bluebells carpeting the woods that she had visited, still looked as colourful as ever. The memories of building dens with her many friends from the estate, not just Jamie, appeared vividly in her mind.

Sue's street gave her a memory from her childhood. It was of a school friend's birthday party. She still had the scar on her knee from falling off a barrel in their garden after balancing on it whilst rolling down a slope. All the memories were still there. She had just let them fade since being a police officer.

Sue's house seemed a lot more in order since the last time they had visited. The entertainment system that they had noticed strewn across the floor had gone. When Heather asked Sue, why they weren't using it, she simply said that it had been faulty, so they had to send it back.

After making Heather a cup of tea, she offered her a seat at the dining table.

'You may want to write down what I have to say next. But could I ask you not to say anything to Dai unless you really have to? I want to tell him myself when the time is right.'

Heather nodded and took out her notepad.

'You see, I have been covering this up for so long, and I don't want Dai to know how many lies I have had to tell to stop him from finding out.'

Heather was expecting Sue to tell her that she was having some torrid affair and not the revelation that she finally came out with.

'A year or so back I was conned out of three hundred pounds by some woman called Red.'

Heather took down all the details. She didn't mention to Sue that her impostor had also been known as Red. She didn't want her to get her hopes up, of finally getting justice. The story was damning. The nerve of the woman, she thought. There still weren't any leads that they could follow-up, but at least they knew that they were looking for a serial fraudster.

Heather assured Sue that she wouldn't mention any of this to Dai, but advised her to tell him herself. She explained that more lies would probably have to be told otherwise. And she needed her help with the case if she could possibly bring herself to relive it.

'I've asked the manager at Sunnyville to visit our forensic artist at the station. Hopefully, we will get an artist's impression of her. They can recreate an image by someone telling them what the person looked like. Do you think you could put one together with one of our artists, Sue? Or do you not remember what she looked like?'

Sue raised her eyebrows. 'I wish I could forget what she looked like. That woman has caused me nothing but pain since the first moment I laid eyes on her. I will help with the sketch.'

It wasn't a photograph, but it was the next best thing. If these sketches matched up, then they could confirm that they were looking for the same woman. The squad would pull apart the information that Sue had given. Considering that this all started on the school drop off at Beechwood primary, meant there may be a chance that she lives on the estate, or has relatives there. She had a good feeling about this. She would suggest that they begin the search for Red there.

When Heather eventually made it over to Martha's, she was still unsure of whether to mention that she had spent time with Jamie. She had told Martha about her in the past and had also mentioned that she had once broken her heart.

They had spent today talking about Jamie's personal life, of which was none of Martha's business.

Heather knew Sarah, and how much in love the two were. It was simply heartbreaking to find out the terrible news. That beautiful family had been on her mind all day. She had also been thinking of Jamie. She knew it was selfish of her, but she couldn't help it. Something inside her still had a longing for the woman. She had buried all feelings for her deep inside since their marriage.

She had been happy for them both. She knew that Sarah would look after Jamie and be all she had ever wanted in a woman. But now Sarah was gone, and she was still here.

'Heather—Heather—I said do you want to take the dogs down to the beach with me? Blow off some of the stresses of the day.'

Martha had woken her from her daydream. She had been sitting on the veranda overlooking the sea.

'Yeah, sure, I'll be there now.'

She watched Martha at the bottom of the stone steps getting the dogs ready. Soon they would be jumping through the waves, catching sticks and losing the balls that Martha would throw.

She watched as Martha placed their towels on the wall ready to use after their hosing down. It truly was a beautiful place to live, and she loved it when sleeping over. Hearing the waves crash against the rocks and watching the sun come over the sea was like being on a holiday that you didn't have to go home from. It was so peaceful compared to her little flat.

She would love to live at the beach house full time. But with the thoughts of Jamie clouding her mind, it made her realise that her feelings for Martha may not be as strong as when she had nursed her back to health.

'Come on Heather, they are getting restless.'

The dogs bounded through the gate, kicking up a mound of sand behind them. They headed straight down to the water, just as she had anticipated.

Martha watched the dogs for a moment, then her eye was drawn to the woman sunbathing by the wall. As Heather approached, she noticed that Martha hadn't taken her eyes off the woman's glistening, tanned body.

'Getting a good eyeful are you there, Martha?'

She abruptly looked away. 'I don't know what you're talking about. I was just watching the dogs.'

She knew that Martha was feeling a little tied down, too. She was used to having quick flings with women and never being the one committed to a relationship.

As they strolled along the beach, the talk had been about work. It was always about work. She had told her about Sue Evans being conned and about the profile that they had put together of the woman suspected. Unlike Jamie, she was convinced that it would be the same woman doing both the money and the murder. It was a cut-and-dried case to her.

When the police sketch artist had finished with his impressions, it was still hard to tell if it was the same woman. The sketch that Sue had compiled had been a woman with long, curly red hair and the brightest blue eyes. The second picture from the manager at Sunnyville had the woman with straighter red hair, tied back and green eyes. Heather thought that the manager's one looked a lot like the real Sue Evans passport photo. It was uncanny.

The police distributed the sketches around the local papers, and they conducted a soft enquiry to the trusted locals on the Beechwood estate. No one seemed to know the woman.

Staff from the coffee shop that Sue and Red had visited were also asked if they had remembered seeing the woman, or if they had seen her since, but still, the answer was no.

The Wellview clinic was now a nail bar. They had put out an enquiry for its previous staff to contact the police but, as the clinic had disbanded due to government cutbacks, they weren't holding out much luck.

Heather kept thinking of the name Red. It was niggling away at her. She had a slight recollection that someone had mentioned it as a nickname somewhere. She had gone through all the files regarding women that fitted the descriptions given, but there was nothing that jumped off the page at her. Then she realised. The girl that Sue had mentioned had only been in her early twenties. She was looking for someone pushing forty like the actual Sue Evans. She would go back to the beginning and start looking at the juvenile records as well.

## Chapter Seven

Ruby had no intention of killing again. She had gotten away with two murders, thanks to her brother's confession. She had hoped that she could leave her past behind and that her life would take on a fresh path.

Chloe's visit had charred her plans for an easier life. She didn't want to get back in contact with her dark side. But she also knew that unless she entertained Chloe's request, she would never be able to rest.

Chloe knew everything. She was with her at the time she killed her father. She had also clearly stated that she wouldn't mind being charged as an accessory to murder, as at least they would be together. Just like old times. Ruby was sure that Chloe had lost her marbles. How the fuck was she going to kill this Brian arsehole? She kept her victims to family members. Who was Brian, anyway? She thought.

Ruby had googled the name and found Brian on the internet. By the look of him, he wasn't that far away from a heart attack, anyway. Maybe she should just encourage Chloe to make his life hell and just sit and wait. Who was she trying to kid? Chloe couldn't wait for a drive-through takeaway, let alone a calculated murder. She would have to think of something quick.

She tapped her pen on her desk as her lecturer continued with his boring monologue. How would she do it? Poisoning was her thing. She had poisoned both of them. Her father and her stepfather. But how would she get that close to boring Brian? She thought.

Last time, with Phil, she had fallen for him herself. Then, when he refused her, she couldn't take the rejection. He had to go. This time there was no way she was going to waste her time charming this fat fucker. She would have to use a more subtle approach. Was she the type to shoot him? She had never held a gun before, but maybe she could get some lessons, she thought. It would be clean and easy, but not like she had suggested to Chloe. She would shoot him and blame it on someone else. Chloe maybe? No, that would be too messy. They would start digging up their past and Chloe would drop Ruby in it from a big height. Just as she had promised.

She racked her brain and could only come to one conclusion. She would deal with the root of the problem. Chloe must die in his place.

Silencing her from spouting about her past was the only way she could go back to a normal life. Well, her idea of normal anyway. This sounded a more sensible idea, she thought. She didn't know how she would do it, but Chloe had to die.

She lifted her head out of her law books. This was the last year of studying for her degree and soon she would be making enough money to get out of this place, anyway. She didn't need Chloe's money.

The lecturer had finished, and she hadn't heard a word he had said until he waved at her to join him. 'Ruby, would you mind coming down to the front please before you leave?'

What now? She thought. She had already given him a blow job for a better grade. Surely, he wasn't going to go back on the deal. Luckily for her, this was not the case. It seemed he wanted to keep their little meet-ups active.

'I've been thinking. It won't be long before you finish here, and I would miss our little get-togethers. Have you any plans as to what you might do?' The tutor wasn't a bad-looking man, and she knew that he had his uses. 'I have a lot of connections, you know. I could help you out if you want to stay in the area.'

She smiled at him. All she wanted to do was to keep him happy until she passed and then let him down, not so gently. 'Thank you, Mr Wesley. Yes, that would be so helpful. Sorry, but I have to go. My brother will be waiting for me to pick him up from football practice.' She pivoted on her heel and left.

Her brother wasn't waiting for her. Nobody was. She just didn't want to be letched over anymore today. She had more important things to think about. If she was to murder Chloe, she would have to plan this to the last letter.

Chloe was stupid, but not stupid enough to be lured away somewhere for her to do away with her and hide the body.

She would find out more about her. Find out who would miss her or even look for her if she just wasn't around anymore. Her brother Wayne was still in prison and Kevin was living with his boyfriend somewhere. Chloe had said that she hadn't seen him in years, but he may be back to contest the will. She needed to know if there were any appointments that she would have to attend where a no-show would raise suspicion. She would leave no stone unturned. It would have to be a very long time before anyone missed her. That way, she could leave college and start her life elsewhere.

She rang the number that Chloe had given her, and the girl answered on the second ring. They arranged to meet up for a drink in an hour. Chloe had told her that she was working a night shift at the hospital later, which surprised her. After a second thought, she guessed that she may have been a cleaner or a kitchen worker.

The pub she had chosen was dark and usually quiet. She had stolen a baseball cap from the college and pulled it down over her face. If ever there was an investigation into Chloe's disappearance, she didn't want to be recognised like the last time.

Chloe arrived wearing navy scrubs. Ruby had underestimated her, she thought. She hadn't seen the girl in years, but had never expected her to be a nurse. Chloe had noticed her surprised expression and felt dismayed.

'What's that look for? Did you think I was too thick to be a critical care nurse? You need to close your mouth; you look like you're catching flies.' She signalled over to the barman and asked if he could bring them two whiskeys, then flounced down hard in the chair.

'I know that I shouldn't say anything but fuck me, it's hard listening to people moan all night.'

Ruby slowly sipped away at her whisky, but Chloe downed hers in one. 'That's better. Right, have you had time to think about my proposition? Are we going to send Brian on his merry way or what?'

Ruby thought that Chloe was simply a deranged fool. Every time she saw the girl, it was like she had a different personality. The problem was, which personality would she be using when Ruby attempts to send *her* on her merry way?

Maybe this wouldn't be as easy as she first thought. The girl had some balls to come and break into her home like that. What if she had called the police or had hit her with that iron-based lamp? She was precarious and unpredictable. She would have to make her think that it was her idea.

'I've thought long and hard about this, and I think you were right. We should pretend to rob the bank. I haven't planned anything yet but I'm sure that we can set something up.'

Chloe looked intrigued. This was worth downing another whisky for. She signalled to the barman and looked back at Ruby. 'Go on.'

'Well, first we need to learn how to shoot. We can't do it here, or ours would be the first door that the police would knock on. We need to go away for a bit, to a firing range or something. Could you do that with work? And friends and family? Would they miss you? Do you have appointments planned?'

'Fuck me, Ruby, slow down. This is some crazy shit you're spouting. But no, no fucker would miss me. My mam and fucking Brian never want me anywhere near them, so if I didn't turn up to visit they would think that I'd got the message and just fucked off somewhere. My shrink would think the same. I have appointments booked with her, but she knows how bad I am at remembering appointments.'

'What about work? I'm guessing a critical care nurse couldn't just up and leave whenever she felt fit.'

Chloe laughed out loud. 'Did you really believe I was a nurse? I stole this from the changing rooms when I was in there picking up my meds. I just walked onto the ICU ward last night and nobody, I'm saying nobody questioned me.'

Ruby shook her head. Her first impression was right. The girl was off-the-scale crazy.

'Tonight, I'm going back there, and I'm going to go through the patient's wallets.'

Ruby shook her head again. She couldn't believe what she was hearing.

'What? They will probably be dead by the morning, it's critical care. They ain't going to complain about a few quid going missing, are they?'

The girl was deranged. If she had a brain cell, it would be lonely. Chloe would end up inside herself if she kept on with this drama. Ruby had decided that bumping her off would put her out of her misery.

'So, no one would come looking for you if we spent some time away?'

'Well, the cat would miss me, but I'm sure the old lady across the street is feeding him. He's so fucking fat, you ought to see him. I can't afford to feed him that much. He sat on her car bonnet the other day, lazing in the sun like he was fucking Garfield. I'm sure that he smirked at me as well.'

Ruby interrupted. 'OK, the cat may miss you. What about Kevin? Does he ever visit? Or does he expect you to turn up for a meeting about the will?'

She laughed again hysterically this time.

'He wouldn't piss on me if I was on fire. He never liked me when I was a kid. I think it was because he wanted to wear my dresses. What d'ya reckon? Fucking gay boy. Frankie should have done something about that when he had the chance.'

Ruby reminded her that Frankie had. 'Well, he did disown him, didn't he? I don't know why you're worried about him getting Frankie's money. I bet Frankie put something in a will or told some solicitor that he was to be left with nothing.'

Chloe nodded. She was probably right. 'As it stands though, if we don't see off Brian, he will be in charge of Frankie's money anyway and we still won't get a penny.'

Ruby cocked her eyes. 'Yes, I know that. That's why we have to sort it out. Can you get hold of a gun? Nothing special just something that would scare the fuck out of someone if it was pointed at them. You never know it may cause him to have a heart attack and we wouldn't have to bother actually shooting the prick.'

'No fucking way. I'm not going to be the one to be phoning up Frankie's contacts and asking for a gun. We will have to see if someone on the estate can get us one. We are going to do this then are we? Definitely, now you're not going to back out on me or anything?' Chloe was quite shocked that she had managed to blackmail her old friend.

'No Chloe, I'm not going to back out of it. Look, it's half-term next week. I'll tell my mam that I'm going away with a friend from campus. She won't know any different.'

Chloe was content. The thought of Brian being six feet under gave her a sense of ownership. All she needed to do was to find out where he would be and when, so they could plan the perfect murder.

The house was as cheery looking as ever. A place for everything and everything in the place that Brian had demanded it should be. She could hear the sounds of Radio 2 coming from the back garden, so went through the large iron gate.

She watched as Brian's fat arse bent down to attend to his plants and she imagined him sprawled out cold on the floor. She called out to him. He had heard her, but ignorantly waited a while before replying.

'Chloe, why are you here? You've lost your job, is that it?' Brian carried on watering the plants. He didn't even bother to look up at her. 'Your mother's not here. She's at work—where you should be.'

The girl stood there. The garden shears were lying on the ground next to him. She could quite easily stab the bastard or cut off his fucking head and limbs like a branch from a big fat tree, she thought, but no. She would wait for Ruby's help. She only came to see him, as he wasn't at the bank. She wasn't concerned about him or anything like that, she just wanted to find out his work pattern.

'So why ain't you at work, dear Step Daddy?' Brian shrugged off the sarcasm.

'I am in the process of retiring Chloe, not that it's any of your business. Your mother and I are thinking of moving to Spain when it's all finalised. Didn't she mention it? No, you haven't bothered to phone her in weeks, so I suppose not.'

Keeping in contact works both ways, she thought. Her mother never bothered to ring her, so she had given up being the one that always stayed in contact.

'So, does this mean that you are not going back to the bank then?'

'No, you silly girl. I have to go back until I retire. I'm just having a peaceful day in the garden. Well, it was peaceful until you turned up.'

She hated the man, but still, she thought she would have one more attempt to reason with him. 'Look, Brian, I'm in a much better place in my head now. I don't need you to be taking care of my finances anymore. I want to prove to everyone that I can stand on my own two feet. They made you my power of attorney because I couldn't hold myself together, but I'm better now.'

The man looked at her this time. He wanted to make his words heard. They had made him the power of attorney for a reason. If he hadn't, she would have been dead by now. The suicide attempts meant that she had spent a lot of time in the hospital. He had to step in. There was no other choice.

'How in God's name can you say that you are better, Chloe? The last psychiatrist you saw is still waiting for an apology for trashing his office. Do you know how much money it cost to replace that bloody fish tank? He had fish in there that were worth hundreds of pounds.'

Chloe rolled her eyes. Here we go, she thought, another fucking lecture.

'I'm running out of people that will take you on. It was conditional that you kept up with your therapy, but you haven't. You may not be slitting your wrists anymore, but you are killing what is left of your brain with that shit that you are shoving up your nose.'

Chloe shuffled awkwardly.

'You thought that we didn't know about that, didn't you? What baffles me is where you are getting the money from to pay for it.'

It was useless trying with him. Yes, she had used stuff to make her feel halfway normal sometimes, but she wasn't an addict. She wouldn't let herself get addicted. All she wanted was to take back control of her life. There was no way they would ever give her Frankie's money if he was still in charge of her. With him gone, and her mother taking over, she knew that she could change her mother's mind.

'Maybe I could help with the garden? I could prove to you that I'm not a total waster. Are you back at work next week? I could come around when you're not here, so I don't get on your nerves.'

Brian couldn't believe the audacity of the girl. 'Yes, I am. I don't leave until the end of the month. But if you think that I am going to let you loose in this garden, you must be crazier than I thought you were. Go home, Chloe. Sort yourself out. I will let you know when I find another psychiatrist to take you on. Until then, stay out of trouble.'

He had done it. He had signed his death certificate. She was slowly having second thoughts about killing the bastard, but now she had made up her mind. He was never going to let her live her own life. So, she would end his. The only regret she would possibly have after committing the deadly deed was how his death may affect her mother. Even after everything she had done. The denial she had faced when mentioning the abuse from Frankie and choosing Brian over her hadn't changed the love she had for her mother.

She was the only one that understood her rages when she was younger. She was always out on the estate, shouting the odds and defending her daughter. Everyone knew not to mess with Joan Fisher.

When she waved Frankie goodbye for his time inside, she made damn sure that she wouldn't succumb to all the gossip on the estate dragging her down. She had stood on her own two feet before and would do it again.

The Fishers had been one of the first families on the estate when it was first built in the 1960s. There were over four thousand tenants on the council waiting list, and Newport was building five hundred houses a year. Three thousand were to be put on the estate nestled amongst the countryside. Many of the families thought it to be the poshest estate in Newport, as the houses had inside toilets and both front and back gardens.

The Fisher's had thought of themselves as going up in the world when they moved there. Joan had been known as the typical *quiet girl next door*. It shocked everyone how a girl like her would have wound up with the wannabe gangster Frankie Thompson. Her parents had lost all respect for her when she let herself get pregnant so young. Especially to a married man.

Brian knew nothing of their past. When he moved them off the estate to Cardiff, Joan ditched all of her old friends from the estate. The wife of a respected bank manager had a reputation to hold up.

Chloe had decided that in the long run, her mother would be able to cope. She would pull herself together and make sure of it. She would take her away with Frankie's money and they could start anew somewhere else, as the close mother-and-daughter unit that they once were.

Chapter Eight

When Kate finally agreed to let the detectives in for a quick meeting, she stipulated her terms before they stepped foot inside the door. It would have to be quick, as she had a busy schedule and could not change her plans. Heather couldn't believe the cheek of the woman. According to her, nobody else in the world was as important as her.

When they entered her home, it was the same chilly reception as before. She and Shane were unwelcome visitors. They had tried several times to get hold of the woman and there were a lot of important things to discuss. They had left messages on her mobile and house phone. They had even left messages at the surgery, but nothing. Not so much as a word of concern. So, turning up outside her house unannounced was their last attempt at contact.

'I do understand what you're saying, Detective, and you may be ready to release the body, but have you caught the person who took the money?'

Heather was concerned that Kate had been more interested in the money than in who murdered her father.

'Miss Thomas, we needed to meet with you to establish what will happen next to your father's body. The coroner needs to release the body to a funeral director of the family's choice. Then he can issue a burial or cremation order. The coroner will still be investigating the circumstances surrounding the death, but at least you can plan the funeral.'

The woman scowled her face. 'And how do you suppose that I pay for the funeral, detective? Whoever stole that bank card should be the one paying for his funeral. There were at least a thousand pounds taken.'

Heather could feel how irate the woman was getting with every word that she rather loudly uttered.

'Did your father have life insurance, Miss Thomas? Surely with his age, it would have been enough for a decent burial.'

Kate Thomas tried to avoid the question. She had stopped paying the premiums, as she was hoping that the state would pay for the funeral when all of his money was gone. She wasn't expecting to still be in the country at the time of his death.

When her husband left her for their hired hand, she had been distraught. She didn't fight to keep him, as that wasn't her style. Letting him go and having to pay him for half of their family home had crippled her. But it was a small price to pay to keep her self-respect.

The gambling had started out of boredom. The nights in front of the TV, alone, downing bottles of wine had become tedious. She would scroll on her phone for hours pursing her lips at all the pictures of happy couples on social media while she downed another bottle in jealousy. Then, without realising what she had done, she had made herself a gambling account.

At first, it was a few games of blackjack just to pass the lonely hours. Later came the slots. She would sit with a glass of wine in one hand and the other, hitting the button again and again. The pounds would disappear before her eyes. Before she realised how far it had taken her, she had emptied her savings account.

She would never have thought of herself to be the type to gamble. She was too middle class. But betting secretly on her phone had become a need. The game companies were giving away hundreds of free bets just to get you to sign up for an account with them. And occasionally she would actually win. The feeling of winning would consume her, even if it was short-lived. But it wasn't long before she realised that nothing had actually been given away for free. The free bets had been used to entice her; drawing her in and squeezing her dry.

It wasn't long before she had created hundreds of separate online gambling accounts. As soon as she ran out of credit, she would simply go to another site and open a new one. She had also opened up credit card accounts in her father's name, and five high-interest payday loans. These were in her ex-husband's name, so she didn't mind defaulting on them. When the statements came through the door, she would simply send them back, stating not known at this address.

When it finally hit her that her gambling had taken over her every thought, she was adamant that if she bet larger amounts, she could win the money back. But before she knew it, she was paying out her month's wages to creditors and credit cards.

Fearing the bailiffs knocking on her door, she reluctantly put her house up for sale. But refused to have a for sale sign outside of the property. When it first went on the market, it had started getting views. There were even a few offers made. The reason that the offers hadn't moved from the table, was her. Every time she spoke to a potential buyer, she couldn't bring herself to be civil to them. She was losing the one thing that she had saved from her ten-year marriage, and her pride wouldn't allow her to go through with it.

At first, she had tried to change its appearance. But making it less appealing to her had got her even more frustrated. The kitchen she chose to put in, she hated. She thought that if she did this, she could detach herself from the property. The plan didn't work. All it did was get her into even more debt, with the workman carrying out the changes.

Everyone was on her back for money. But the only money she had was tied up in the house. She had also spent most of her father's money. He no longer had any savings, and the care home was being paid for by his weekly pension. The fact that someone had got their greedy little hands on the only money he had in his personal account had turned her stomach. She refused point blank to pay for his care. The care home had since been chasing her for the last payments before he died. She thought this was an insult, as he died in their care, so they really shouldn't be asking for any money.

Heather was unaware of her unfortunate predicament, and Kate Thomas was determined to keep it that way.

'What if I say to you that I don't want to take any responsibility for my father's body? I mean—what would happen if I simply walked away from this?'

The statement took Heather by surprise. She didn't really have a straightforward answer. If his daughter had been the one in charge of his care up to now, she didn't see how or why she would want to detach her responsibility like that.

'Miss Thomas. You need to consider every option that is open to you before you make any rash decisions. We will leave it here for today. Give you some time for your grief to rationalise.'

This was nothing to do with grief. She had wished the old bastard dead many times. He had been the same as her ex-husband. He was always waiting for the next piece of skirt to turn his head. Her mother had led a dog's life with his philandering ways. She was adamant about not ending up like her; taking her own life at fifty. The bastard could rot in the coroner's office for all she cared.

'This is my decision, DI Williams. I am not laden with grief, as you can probably tell. My relationship with my father was not a loving one. I just want his arrangements taken care of without my input.'

Heather could see that the woman had made up her mind. As cold and as callous as it may have seemed, the woman would surely have had her reasons.

'OK Miss Thomas, if this is the case, then a public health funeral will need to be arranged by the local authority. If Mr Thomas has any money in his estate, the amount will then be recovered.'

Kate Thomas swallowed hard before commenting on this. She had spent all of his money. She had also sold his belongings off and used the money to pay off her immediate debtors. She was hoping to have sold her house and moved away by the time anyone came looking, but this hadn't been the case.

'Are you sure that there are no other relatives that may want to arrange your father's funeral? When we first met, you seemed to have thought that there was an illegitimate son somewhere. Would you have a name and an address, so that we could perhaps contact him?'

'I'm sure that there are many bastards of his out there, but sadly I have never met any. So no, DI Williams, I cannot help with this one. Throw him in a ditch for all I care.'

Heather was bewildered as to why the woman had felt that strongly. 'Miss Thomas, I understand that you do not want anything more to do with the funeral, but you will still need to help with the financial side of things. Am I right in thinking that your father had a property?'

Kate Thomas shook her head in disbelief at the personal questions that Heather was asking. She made her way to the front door and stood there with it open.

'I think it's time that you leave now, please. This is becoming much too personal for me, and I would rather appoint someone else to deal with your questions.'

Heather could see that she was getting nowhere with the woman, so did as she asked.

When they left, Kate went to the bottom of the stairs and sat down. This was it. This was the moment she had been dreading. She had sold her father's house already. She had forged his signature and used the money to pay off the payday loans she had accrued. The power of attorney she had in place was only for his health and welfare decisions and not for his property and financial affairs. When she made enquiries about adding the property and financial side to her responsibilities, they began asking too many questions, so she didn't follow it through. Les Thomas had a wealthy pension. He was a well-respected physician back in his day. There was no need to sell off his property just yet.

As soon as Les Thomas had a few falls at home, he rented out his house and went to live with his daughter on the understanding that as soon as he was well enough, he would move out. The two of them had argued to the point of despair, and neither of them wanted the arrangement to continue. When she put the idea of Sunnyville into his head, he thought it would be on a short-term basis. He had accepted that he could stay there until they had a system sorted out with visiting carers easing the load. That way, they could go back to spending as little time as possible together.

Kate Thomas had other ideas. She wanted to sell the house straight away so they wouldn't have the burden of it when he went into care, but he refused. He had his reasons to keep hold of the house and had hoped to be living back there one day.

An old acquaintance of Les had recommended the tenants that were renting the place. When Les found out who they were, the family lawyer drew up an open-ended contract. It stipulated that they would only have to leave if he sold the property. Les Thomas had made that decision when he was in sound mind and the property was not to be sold under any circumstance.

When the tenancy was finalised, she took all of his belongings and put them into storage. This was apart from a locked suitcase whose contents intrigued her. It sounded like paperwork when she gave it a shake. She still hadn't found the deeds to the house so made sure that she would take it back and have a rummage through.

The contents caused another dent in their father-and-daughter relationship as she came across her father's personal letters. Some were from her mother. She struggled to read their contents as she had it confirmed that her mother's suicide was down to his philandering ways.

The next set of letters was from Allison McKenzie. She had been his receptionist at the hospital. Kate had remembered the name distinctly from her childhood. They were clearly love letters and as soon as she realised this; she stopped reading. She tied them back up in the bundle, the same way that she had found them, then put them back in the case.

The next discovery was the contract the tenants had signed for the house. It was in the name of Mr James McKenzie. There were also papers declaring Mr McKenzie's DNA match with her own father.

The letter that was with the documents had Allison McKenzie's handwriting on it. The woman had begged her father to look after his son's wellbeing. It explained that the woman was ill, and as she didn't have long left to live; she had requested the help of Les Thomas. The nature of the letter suggested that the news of his parental responsibility had been a shock. A well-kept secret that had been kept from the boy for all of his life. The woman also stated that she wished for James McKenzie to not be told of his parentage. He had lived his life with a loving father that he had thought of as his own and she wanted it kept that way. The only thing she wanted from Les Thomas was the financial stability of a family home.

At first, it was apparent by the nature of the returning letters, that Les Thomas would have wanted to tell the man that he was his father. He had also mentioned that he would have liked to strike up a relationship with his grandchild, but Alison McKenzie was adamant that she didn't want her son to have any knowledge of their affair. She only needed him financially, as she wouldn't be able to leave the man with any inheritance.

When Kate met up with her half-brother, she felt no connection. She just saw him as someone that was in the way of her getting on with her own life. She explained to the man that her father couldn't afford to keep the house on as he needed money to pay for the care home. James McKenzie and his wife had felt sorry for her father. They understood the situation and would leave with no questions asked. His mother had recently died, and the council had allowed him to take on her house as a family home. This was the place that had been his family home growing up, so they moved on quite quickly.

Kate was the only one still keeping their sordid little secret and now that she had sold the property, she didn't need anyone else trying to get their hands on his empty estate. She had no idea how she was going to carry on with the web of lies that she had weaved whilst hiding away her gambling habit. Coming clean and admitting it all was not an option. The embarrassment would be too much to bear.

She would have to forge another letter granting her permission to sell. She would backdate it and use it if she was ever in the position of being accused of fraud. If he had died in his sleep like he was supposed to, she wouldn't have had to deal with all the added pressure of an investigation taking place. She could have just buried him at a council estate funeral and left no forwarding address to be contacted at for them to reclaim the money. But no, he had stayed alive just to spite her. Sunnyville, was still calling her every week for her to come and visit, and all she wanted was a call to say that he had passed.

Her life was a mess, but she wouldn't let the bastards win. Her ex-husband and her dead father would have always expected her to fail. Not this time, she thought. She would find a way to dig herself out of the debt and go back to the respected medical receptionist that she saw herself as.

As the estate agents put the for sale sign up, outside her house, Kate Thomas complained that it was leaning too much to the left. If the eyesore was to be standing in front of her house, it would at least look like it was standing up straight.

## Chapter Nine

When Ruby raised her head from Mr Wesley's lap, she caught him looking at his watch.

'What the fuck? Are you checking the time, Wesley? Making sure that we get in on time, is it? You've already broken the rules by being out in the car park with a student sucking you off. I don't think you need to worry about your lateness.'

The man quickly did up his trousers and reached over to the back seat to get his case. Ruby noticed the stag key ring that was hanging from the mirror, and it gave her an idea.

'Do you still go shooting on the weekends, Mr Wesley? I'd love to come and watch how you cock your rifle.'

The man was quite pleased that the girl was giving him attention. 'Well, yes, I am, and if you would like to come, I can always pick you up in the morning. Maybe we could go for a spot of lunch and park up somewhere.'

The dirty bastard, she thought. She knew what park up meant and there was no way she would ever go that far with him. She only wanted to get hold of his rifle. She could pinch it when he wasn't looking and hide it somewhere. Then, when he dropped her off, she could drive back for it. It would be easy for her to get Chloe to come with her in the car if she thought that they were going to practice at a firing range with a real rifle. All she needed then was a place to bury the body. That would be another thing. Getting a spade to dig with and finding some soft ground.

She knew how hard it was to bury a body. Phil's grave had already been dug when she took off the topsoil and put him in it. She had Jack to help her then as well. This time, she would be on her own. But Chloe would be gone, and she could start to live some sort of honest life. One without a ghost around every corner trying to tempt her back to her evil ways. It had to work. It was her only chance, she thought.

Wesley had taken Ruby to a wooded area at the side of the mountain. He had told her that it was good for shooting rabbits and that he had also shot the odd deer to amuse himself. Ruby wasn't impressed with the killing of any defenceless animals. To her, it was barbaric. She was impressed at how well he had held the gun, though.

'Let me have a go, Wesley.'

She took the gun from him, and the man instantly knew that he should have insisted that she didn't. She was waving it around in front of his face and making him very nervous.

'Give it back, Ruby. I will teach you how to load it and shoot something, but you must treat the gun with respect.'

She handed it back and watched as he carefully loaded the rifle before explaining the rules.

'You must always have the safety catch on. This locks the trigger and prevents accidents. You need to keep this on, right until it's time to shoot.'

Ruby watched with intensity. When he gave the loaded gun back to her, she could feel her blood rising to the surface. She was excited. The thought of instantly ending someone's life had appealed to her. No more waiting to see if a heart had stopped beating.

Wesley lined up a few cans on a fallen log and held onto Ruby. He moved in close behind her, manoeuvering the rifle, hand over hand, to get into the firing position. When he moved gently back, she fired. The reaction nearly had her off her feet, but she had hit her target.

'I did it. I fucking did it.' She began waving the gun around in the air. Wesley weaved around the girl to make sure that he was standing behind it.

'Ruby, you're a natural. It took me ages to get my first hit.' He went in for a kiss, but she turned away from him and fired again. This time, she missed.

'That was you, putting me off.' She spun around and waved the gun in his face. He managed to duck underneath it and quickly moved behind her again. He gently took the rifle from her hands and began to pack it away.

'That's enough for today, Ruby. Let's put this back in the car and have that picnic. Yeah?'

After the picnic, Ruby loaded the car with the remainder of the food as Wesley went to find a tree to relieve himself on. She took the opportunity to take the rifle and a box of shots out of the boot and hid them behind a fallen tree that was at the edge of the clearing.

Lucky for Ruby, Wesley hadn't bothered to check whether the gun was in the boot. He was more interested in trying to persuade her to get in the back of the car with him. She made up an excuse that it was getting late and told him to take her home.

When they returned, she jumped out of his car and into hers. The plan was to pick up a spade and some black bin bags from a hardware store and get back to find the rifle.

The plan had worked well. All Ruby had to do was find the rifle that she had hidden in the trees. She could then re-hide it a few miles away, along with the spade. It would have to be somewhere remote with soft ground.

There were plenty of mountains around. All she had to do was convince Chloe to go for a little drive. She would tell her they were going somewhere to practice and then she could end all of this madness. She would bury her secrets along with the girl that she had known all her life.

Poor Chloe, she thought. She's going to wish that she had never broken into her house and confronted her.

Ruby had some planning to do. But first, she had to find that bloody rifle and the box of shots she had hidden.

It had taken her ages to find the place again. The lanes all looked the same, and there were hardly any landmarks to remember. It was all countryside.

It was getting dark, and she was shitting herself out there alone. She couldn't go back, in case Wesley came to look for it.

After what seemed like hours, she found the clearing. With the nightlife of the forest giving her goosebumps from every shriek and sound, she made her way to the fallen tree.

When she rummaged around in the dry leaves, a field mouse ran up her arm. She screamed, then after a few shivers composed herself. She would have to put her hand back in there and find what she came for. After another attempt, she felt the cold metal and prized the gun out from the undergrowth.

With the darkness closing in, it was now too late to drive far. She would have to change her plans and hide the rifle closer.

She drove the car to the next clearing and hid the rifle inside an old, rotting tree. She positioned the car so that the headlights could guide her way through the trees. There was a spot with a soft patch of dirt. This would be perfect, she thought.

She began digging. The sweat was dripping off her head, and she wiped it away with her hands full of dirt. Her clothes were also full of mud, but she couldn't stop. She would change when she got home and put her clothes through the wash before her mother asked any questions.

When she finished, she sat on the edge, gazing into the hole. This was really happening. This would be the end of her nightmare, she thought.

The next morning, she called Chloe and told her to get her walking boots on for their adventure. They arranged to meet for breakfast, and Ruby told her some of the plans. She explained that the rest would be a surprise.

At first, Chloe looked a bit sceptical. But knowing she was spending the day in the company of her old friend made her start looking forward to it.

The girls had sung all the way. They both knew every lyric to *When the sun goes down* by the Arctic Monkeys and had kept it on repeat.

Ruby had actually enjoyed Chloe's company, and she hers. They had talked about everything but their past. They had left that well and truly alone. Chloe was feeling as if she finally had someone in her life that would understand her crazy ways. Ruby, being a deranged double murderer, seemed to top her own life's antics. There was now someone in her life that had done worse things than her. Maybe she could turn a corner herself now. She could stop blaming herself for the bad things in her past and really pull herself together. This would be after they had killed Brian, of course.

'So where is this rifle range, anyway? We seem to be well up in the sticks now.'

Ruby had been waiting for Chloe to ask that question. 'Well, Chloe, I've managed to do better than that. We are not going to a rifle range anymore. I pinched a rifle from Wesley. I thought we'd go somewhere quiet and shoot at some cans.'

Chloe panicked a little. 'Won't he know that it's missing?'

Ruby laughed and told her the story about how she had tricked Wesley. Chloe had found it hysterical. She had called Chloe from his car earlier just to make sure that she kept the morning free.

When she thought about what Ruby had said, she was up for it. She had worried that a rifle range may have been a little too expensive. She had to show Brian exactly what she had spent her measly weekly allowance on, and he didn't allow her any playtime.

Chloe was so looking forward to having her own money. The first thing she had promised herself was a little car like Ruby's. She hadn't passed her test but could drive a car just as well as her brothers. Wayne had taught her when she was younger, as he needed her to hide cars for them.

Brian hadn't allowed her to take her driving test. He said that there was a chance that she would either drink and drive and kill someone or she would drive herself into a tree on purpose and he would have to pay the medical bills.

He had no faith in her ability to do anything. He was always putting her down, saying she was from bad stock, meaning her father. This may have been true. But Brian wasn't a thoroughbred either. He was a fat wimp of a man who would run away from his own shadow if it looked like it needed money from him.

She didn't know what her mother saw in him. To go from Frankie the feared wannabe gangster to Brian, the man with three chins in a suit from the eighties, seemed unthinkable. He was even too tight to spend any money on himself, let alone on anyone else.

He had calculated every penny that he had ever spent on Chloe. He had written it down as an IOU for her to pay him back. If she was ever to get any inheritance from Frankie, the money that he had given St Hilda's and all the psychiatrist's bills would have to be accounted for.

Brian had already started dipping his fat fingers in the pot with her disability benefit. It's a small drop in the ocean of debt that you owe me, my girl, he would say.

Others may have thought that he was the doting father replacing the waster that she had had previously. She knew differently.

Since day one, he made sure that she knew that she wasn't wanted. She had always been the mess that he had had to clear up and put away. He didn't tell any of his friends about her, but Chloe made sure that she would drop in on him now and then, just to cause a stir.

She loved being the unwanted guest at his golf dinners. She would pull up a spare chair and call him Daddy just to make sure that everyone knew that they were related. Her favourite though, was the bank. If he had an important meeting, she would turn up, pressing her nose against the window; pulling faces at him through the glass to make sure he knew that she was still around.

Ruby drove past the clearing she had been in with Wesley and knew that hers was the next on the left. 'This seems like a good place.'

Chloe agreed, and they both checked to make sure that there were no other cars around. The spade, black bin bags, and the Chloe-shaped hole weren't far away. She had watched on a tv crime show that it was always better to wrap the body in a black bin bag, so animals didn't get the scent and start digging. She needed that tip and wanted to be as far away from this place before anyone came looking.

She took the rifle and started to head into the trees. After a few minutes, Chloe was feeling anxious, and Ruby could tell that there was something wrong.

'I'm not shooting any rabbits' mind or creatures like that. I couldn't cope with having their eyes looking at me.'

Ruby laughed and agreed. It impressed her that Chloe had the same values as her. After all the bad things that these girls had done to people, they would never contemplate hurting an animal.

'Nah, there are plenty of things we can shoot at. We just need to feel like we know what we are doing. When we eventually point at that bastard, we don't want to get all nervous and get caught.'

They moved deeper into the forest. Ruby recognised the area and looked over to where she had stashed the equipment to finish the job.

'This will do.' She put the gun down and kneeled on the floor. Chloe watched with anticipation.

'Do you even know how to load it?'

Ruby shrugged. 'No, not really. But I did spend a day with a twat who did.'

Ruby loaded the rifle. It was now or never. She had gotten this far without any hiccups and breathed a sigh of relief that she had watched Wesley well enough to load the rifle herself.

Chloe was sitting looking at the ground. Ruby called her name and as the girl looked up, she pointed the barrel at her face.

'Get up and start walking over there.'

She waved it in the direction of the grave.

At first, she thought that Ruby was kidding around, but then she saw how serious the moment had become. Chloe put her hands in the air. She tried to mumble out a few words to defend herself, but Ruby laughed at her.

'You didn't think that I would kill Brian for you, knowing that you were still around to blackmail me afterwards. Did you?'

She told her to stop where the spade, black bin bags, and her last resting place would be. Chloe looked over at them and closed her eyes. She had never felt this close to death before and accepted that her time was up.

As Ruby walked towards her, she concentrated a little too much on keeping Chloe in sight. An exposed tree root had made its way into a loop on the ground in front of her. Ruby caught her foot in the middle of it, tripping her to the floor. As she went down, the gun went off.

Chloe still had her hands in the air and didn't want to open her eyes. When she eventually did, she could see the blood pooling around what was left of Ruby's head.

The girl wasn't moving. But it wasn't Chloe's fault. Ruby was going to kill her. She had to get that into her head to think about her next move. She saw the spade and the black bin bags that had been lying in wait to be used for the burial of her own body. The hole had already been dug. All she had to do was drag her into it, but she couldn't. She didn't want anything to do with it. Ruby had come here to kill her. If she buried her, it would be her hiding a body and involving herself with the death. She would just leave everything as it was, without her DNA all over it.

The only thing she would take from the scene was Ruby's car. She had no choice. There was no way she would be running through a forest away from a dead body. She had watched too many horror films to know how that could possibly pan out.

Luckily, Ruby had left the keys in the ignition, probably for her own quick getaway. She would drive back to Newport and leave the car outside Ruby's house.

The girl's coat and beanie hat were also in the car. Chloe put them on and tucked her red hair away. They were of a similar build, so if any cameras picked the car up, they would assume it was Ruby at the wheel.

On the journey back, she couldn't help feeling betrayed. She didn't want Ruby to die. They had been friends and even though she was blackmailing her; she had hoped that they would remain friends when the job was done.

No one knew Chloe like Ruby. They had suffered together. Who could she turn to for help now? Brian would win. He would take the last shred of self-power away from her, and there was nothing she could do to stop him.

When she arrived back at Ruby's house, she saw that her mother, Karen, was home. This would affect her even more than the others, she thought.

When they were kids, she had thought a lot of Karen. Ruby had also told her that Karen had felt the same about her.

Her brain was being its overstimulated self and before she knew it, she was knocking on the door.

'Hi Karen, it's Chloe.'

The woman invited her in with open arms. They shared tea and toast, and Chloe told her all about herself as a critical care nurse. She still had the uniform, so it was the first thing she could think of. Chloe remembered that Ruby had told her mother that she was meeting up with an old friend over the half-term, so she thought she would take the opportunity to check that this was what she believed.

'So how is Ruby? I thought I'd pay you both a visit as I was on the estate.'

'She's doing well. She will be gutted that she missed you. She's gone off with one of her campus friends. Hiking somewhere. She did say, but for the life of me I can't remember where.' Karen held her hand to her chest. 'Little Chloe from next door. I can't believe that you are here. I suppose it's to do with your father's property is it?' Chloe nodded. 'Your old house is still boarded up, along with the other one that he owned. Mind you, I think there are squatters in them. Or druggies. You know what this place is like.'

Chloe just stared at the woman. She looked a lot older than how she remembered her.

'So, how's your mum doing? Is she still with that Brian bloke?'

It amazed Chloe that it had been so long since they had been off the estate and yet she still remembered her family's business.

'Yeah, still with him.'

Karen was jealous in a small sort of way. It seemed that everyone around her was able to keep their men and she had lost two of hers. Three counting her son.

'Ah, that's good then.'

Chloe got up to leave. She had no more to say. Ruby had told her mother that she was going away for a while, so she knew that Karen wouldn't be sending anyone out to look for her just yet. She could work things out in her mind, on how she was going to deal with Ruby's death. She didn't kill Ruby. But Ruby had planned to kill her, and that hurt.

Before going back to her flat, she thought she would take a walk down to the house she grew up in. It was boarded up, just as Karen had said, but she knew how to get into a Beechwood house easily enough.

It was like stepping into her past and no sign of squatters. Things were just how they had left them. She had assumed that when Frankie came out of prison that he would have lived there, but that hadn't seemed to be the case. Her mother had left most of their belongings behind when they moved out to be with Brian. They didn't want Frankie accusing them of taking anything.

She had a look through the drawers and reminisced about a somewhat disturbed time. When Frankie went to prison, it was OK at home for a bit. Her mother had spent a lot of time with her.

The estate still hated them, so it was them against the many. When Brian came along, everything changed. As soon as his fat face was sitting opposite her at the dinner table, she felt alone.

Amongst the typical spare drawer crap, she found a set of keys. They were Frankie's spare set for the haulage yard. She remembered going there with him, and him secretly hiding stuff under the floor. It was the little key with a monkey key ring attached to it. As she twirled it around her fingers, she decided it was a chance she couldn't help herself from taking. She would go to the haulage yard in the search of treasure.

When she got to the yard, it was quiet. There were only a couple of people around and none in the office. She kept herself hidden in the shadows and crawled stealthily under the tarpaulin of one of the lorries. It was facing the office, so she had a clear view of her pathway. She waited until she was sure, then made a run for it.

She crept under the desk and felt her way along the carpet to the underground safe. She amazed herself that after all these years, she knew where to look.

She lifted the edges of the carpet and pulled. It had been steadfast with dirt, but she found the lock. The little monkey key fitted perfectly and with a slight tug, she was in.

Luck was on her side. There were bundles of cash just waiting there for her to take. She unzipped her jacket and stuffed the wads inside. She looked three stones heavier by the time she made it out of there.

Back at her old home, she stashed the notes in a tiny suitcase that she had used for her dolls when she was little. She would stay there overnight and make her way back to her flat in the morning. It was too dodgy walking around the Beechwood estate at night. Too many thieves around.

The next morning, Chloe woke with a startle. She had been dreaming of Ruby and the shooting. Waking up in the room that always gave her nightmares didn't help, either. It was just as terrifying as it always was.

When she remembered her other excursion, she went through the suitcase. She couldn't believe how much money she had found. She knew that a lot of it was probably counterfeit, but it looked genuine enough to an untrained eye. She had taken Ruby's phone with her, as she knew that when someone started looking for her, the phone would be the first thing to trace. She had tried the PIN once but didn't want to block it. Inside the flip cover were her bank card and driving licence. There was also a scrap of paper with four numbers on it. She tried them on the phone again. This time it worked and Chloe was greeted with a photo of Ruby and her dead brother Jack.

She paused for a while, remembering them both at the age they were in the photograph. Pull yourself together, she thought. Both of these people had done her wrong. It was time to climb out of the mess and get on with her life.

Inside her phone's notepad, was a document named pin. Another four numbers were present. Chloe may have been clever, but that was a stupid place to store a PIN, she thought.

The money would help with her next plan. She would move around from place to place for a bit and use the card and phone. It would then appear that Ruby was active and getting on with her break. She may even buy herself a car with the cash and use Ruby's driving licence she thought. She was sure she could copy her looks. After all, she was getting good at being other people. They were a lot more interesting than her. This way she could live another life and not dwell on the depressing one she was given.

Chapter Ten

DI Josh Bennett had been doing his usual routine of licking the chief's arse. It wasn't going to make any difference. He would still put Heather in charge of the new case no matter how hard he had tried.

When he saw Heather, he reluctantly told her that the desk sergeant wanted a word, so she went straight to him instead of the chief.

'DI Williams, we have found something that may interest you. A Mr Wesley came into the station this morning to report his rifle as missing. Apparently, he had been out shooting and had stopped off to have a picnic. When he loaded the car back up, he left the gun behind. He had been back to the place that he thought he had left it and found nothing. We sent an officer with him to have another look over the spot where he thought he had left it and the surrounding areas. This is where they made a grim discovery. They have found a body of a woman. The rifle was lying next to her. The first impression is that she has died from a gunshot wound to the head.'

Heather rubbed her eyes. She had already been working on the Les Thomas case all night and wondered why they were involving her in this and not another detective.

'OK, does the guy have any idea who the woman is?'

'Well, Mr Wesley is a married man and a lecturer at the college. The problem is, he was not alone when he went for the picnic. He had a young lady with him.' He paused, as he knew that the next line would prick Heather's senses. 'The lady was Ruby Lewis.'

Heather tried not to think of it as karma taking control. This girl had made a fool out of the entire force the last time they were in contact with her. It took all her strength to remain professional and not feel relieved that someone had finally fought back.

Everyone knew that Ruby was the actual killer of her two fathers, but as her brother had admitted to the crime, the case was closed. The police force was under strict instruction not to question Ruby, as she was in specialist care. The doctors were afraid that it would delay her recovery. She had suffered several broken limbs and memory loss from a fall from the side of the mountain, but she had survived.

'This may be a stupid question, but are you sure that she's dead? It's just, this is sounding a bit like Déjà vu to me.'

'Well, she hasn't been formally identified yet, but Mr Wesley seems to think that it's her.'

Heather raised her eyebrows. 'Has he admitted to shooting her?'

'No, nothing like that. He seemed as shocked as me to find the body. And that's not all. Next to it was a freshly dug grave, a roll of black bin bags and a spade leaning against the tree.'

This intrigued Heather more. 'Are we thinking that maybe someone disturbed the killer before they got the chance to bury the body, or do you know of another reason?'

The sergeant shook his head. It was a total mystery. Heather picked up her coat, then downed what was left of her cold coffee.

'I'll drive over to the site and take a look. There may be something they may have missed. After all, we are only human. You keep him comfortable, and I'll have a word when I get back.'

The crime scene was just how they had described it. The freshly dug grave was just sitting there waiting for its resident. She managed to take a look at the deceased before she was driven away. The head had been severely damaged but she concluded that it was indeed Ruby. She held no sympathy for the girl, but did have some for her mother, Karen. She had witnessed her distress when the men in her life had died. All of them at the hands of Ruby. Even her brother Jack would not have pulled the trigger on himself if it hadn't been for the love of Ruby.

She couldn't wait to tell Martha. She would be relieved that the one woman who could taint her shining police career was dead.

Heather had decided that she would drop in on her on the way back to let her know the news. She had always worried in the back of her mind that the things she covered up in the past would come back and haunt her through Ruby. The news of her death would put her mind at rest, at least.

As Heather opened the latch on the back gate, she noticed that the dogs were locked in their outhouse. This was unusual for the time of day, as Martha didn't venture far without them.

As she approached the house, she could hear unfamiliar giggling coming from the bedroom.

Not wanting to see what was happening, but curiosity getting the better of her, Heather opened the door.

Martha jumped at the intrusion. 'Heather, what are you doing here?'

The woman that Martha was entangled with, was the one that she had been eyeing up on the beach earlier in the week. She had recognised the dream-catcher tattoo on her thigh.

'For Christ's sake Martha. You could have at least told me you were back to your old tricks. I fucking hate you sometimes.'

As she shut the door on them, she realised that she wasn't heartbroken. She just felt betrayed. She would probably miss the dogs and the beach house more than Martha.

She had loved and left many lovers in her time, but there had only been one that she had regretted leaving, and it wasn't Martha.

She sat in the car and pulled out her mobile. The dial went straight to an answering machine, so she left a message.

*'Hey Jamie, I've had a cow of a day and wondered if you fancied meeting up for a coffee or a drink later?'*

She wasn't expecting to receive a text back so soon.

*Hey Heather, of course. Come to the house. You know the address.*

Of course, she knew the address. She had driven past there enough times just to get a glimpse of the girl that had once stolen her heart. She had made so many wrong decisions in her life and denying her feelings for Jamie had always nagged away at her.

When Heather returned to the station, Shane said that Martha had been trying to reach her. She dismissed the comment and went straight to the interview room.

Wesley was sitting hunched over, picking away bits from a polystyrene cup. Heather felt sorry for him in a pitying sort of way. She felt that he had become one of Ruby's victims without even realising it. But at least he was still alive, she thought. That was a bonus with Ruby's track record.

'Mr Wesley, do you have any idea how Ruby Lewis may have got hold of your gun?'

The man was visibly shaken. His record showed that he hadn't had so much as a parking ticket before, let alone been involved in a murder inquiry.

'She must have taken it out of the back of the car when I went to, you know... pee.'

'So you were taking a leak, and she thought, *ooh I could do with a gun. I'll just leave it here for later.*'

'Well, yes. Exactly that. The more I think about it now, the more it was all about the gun. When we went shooting, she asked me how to load it and I let her have a go at shooting some cans. She seemed excited about it all.'

The cogs in Heather's brain began to turn over. This was more like the Ruby she knew.

'So, the picnic, was that her idea or yours?'

'Mine, I think. I just wanted to park up for a while and spend some time with her. You don't know how hard it is for someone like me to turn down a girl like Ruby. I tried. For God's sake, I tried. In the beginning, I realised that I had made a mistake and tried to break it off. Then she told me that she would tell my wife everything. I had no choice but to keep seeing her. Then it became more of a need to see her.'

Another time Heather would have had an ounce of sorrow for the man, but after witnessing Martha in her uncompromising situation, she just didn't have the patience.

'I'm sure, Mr Wesley, it must have been terrible for you.'

The man could see the look of disgust on Heather's face and owned it. He knew that if he hadn't fallen into her trap the first time, then he could have just walked away with his head held high. This was never to be, though. She wanted better grades and by taking him in her mouth under his desk, she secured them.

'So did the spade belong to you, too?'

The man shook his head vigorously. 'No, I've never seen it before. When we left together, she was still alive. It was also further down the lane to where I was with Ruby. She must have come back up here with someone else. This has nothing to do with me, I swear.'

Heather believed him. But for the life of her, she couldn't work out how this had happened.

\* \* \*

Seeing Jamie was a breath of fresh air. The kids were running around the house, and Jamie was running around after them. She invited Heather in, and they sat at the breakfast bar on high stools.

'I can't believe this is your world now, Jamie. You have adapted to it so well.'

Jamie smiled. This was true, and she knew it. Motherhood had given her life a new kind of purpose and was glad that it had shown.

'I love them, Heather. They are my world. And I am literally all they have, apart from Uncle Mikey. He has them for me sometimes; if I need to have conversations with people over two feet, that is.' They laughed.

'How is Michael? Is he still strutting his stuff as a drag queen at the club?'

'Oh God no. After the time he spent in custody, he decided to give up all the drag and the men. He runs the club for me now and is doing a damn good job of it. Sometimes he dresses up for special occasions, but I think it brings back too many memories for him.'

Jamie moved to fill the kettle and took out two cups from the cupboard. Before the door closed, Heather noticed a mug with Sarah's name on it and felt a sense of sadness. There were also a lot of photos on the fridge door held on by magnets of the once-so-happy family.

After checking on the kids, Jamie made the coffee and placed it in front of her.

'So, tell me about Martha. Are you and her serious?'

Heather raised an eyebrow at the thought of what she had just witnessed. She didn't want to tell Jamie what had happened. She was now questioning whether her time spent with Martha had been that important. But she could kick herself for letting this happen to her again. She had nursed the woman back from the brink of death and now, when she had fully recovered and was back on her feet, she had wasted hardly any time in getting them horizontal again.

Martha couldn't change. It was not in her nature. Deep down, Heather had always known that it would come to this. She could never be trusted.

Heather realised that she had kept Jamie waiting on an answer to the question. So, she offered a simple reply. 'No, it's nothing serious. In fact, I think it may be over.'

Jamie was surprised. She wasn't expecting to hear that Heather was newly single.

Since Sarah, Jamie had not looked twice at another woman. It had been a year, and friends were encouraging her to get out there and meet new people, but she just couldn't. Her friend Sam had tricked her into going on a double date a few weeks back. The girl had been lovely. And most definitely Jamie's type. But all she could think of was, would Sarah approve?

Before Sarah became really ill, they had talked about her wanting Jamie to move on when she died. But she couldn't entertain the conversation. At the time, she was still waiting for a miracle cure. No one would ever replace Sarah in her heart.

Being here with Heather, though, had felt different. It was nice to have a woman's company in the house. She couldn't deny the fact that she had welcomed meeting up with Heather again. She had also felt a few stirrings in the pit of her stomach, but had pushed them aside, thinking it was still too soon.

Sarah had known Heather. She had approved of the woman and respected her for how well she had looked after the Taylor family when they were going through the trial. If Jamie was ever to love again, it would have to be with someone that Sarah would have approved of. They also had a lot of shared history. They were childhood sweethearts, and no one could match the memories that they had both shared. If it wasn't for the way the world was treating them back then, they may have stood a chance of a real relationship.

The conversation between them was easy. Jamie had mainly talked about the kids, and Heather had enjoyed listening. She loved the way her face lit up when she spoke of their achievements. The excitement in her voice showed that she was doing a good job of being their forever parent.

Inevitably, the conversation turned back around to them. Their first meeting after a lot of years had passed had been very heated.

'We should never have left it so long to get back in touch, Jamie.'

Both remembered their intimate reunion, but hadn't talked about it since.

'Well, I think we made up for it on that first night, Heather.'

Heather picked up a takeaway menu that had been left on the counter and fanned it in front of her face. 'Has it got hot in here all of a sudden, or is that just me?'

Both girls were glowing a shade of red. They were feeling embarrassed by the shared memory, but neither regretted their time together.

Heather had lied to Jamie when she told her at the time that it was just a bit of fun. The feelings that she had for her had never really gone away. Just laid dormant. Jamie had been the same. She was devastated when she found out that Heather had a husband. The situation was never really explained to her, and she had felt like a booty call at the time. But this was also when Sarah came into her life. The woman that had been Jamie's everything.

As she reached for her coffee, she knocked the spoon on the floor. They both reached for it and as their hands touched, their eyes locked.

After a few moments, Heather went in for a kiss, but Jamie pulled respectively away.

'I'm sorry, Heather, but I can't. It's not that I don't want to, it's just I have to think of the kids. They don't need to see their mother in the arms of someone else. It will confuse them.'

Embarrassed by the situation, Heather grabbed her things together to leave. 'I'm so sorry, Jamie. I shouldn't have done that. I don't know what I was thinking.'

Jamie grabbed her arm. 'Don't be silly, sit. I don't want you to leave. We know each other too well to get embarrassed over this, surely.'

Heather kept her gaze looking away from Jamie. 'OK, the thing is, I just caught Martha in bed with another woman this afternoon and my feelings are all over the place.'

Jamie put her arm around her. 'I knew there was something up when you came in. I may not have been in your life for a while, Heather, but I can always tell when you are hiding something.'

Heather cringed. Not only had she made an unprovoked lurch toward Jamie, but she had also covered her true feelings by spurting out what had happened with Martha. She wanted to tell Jamie how she was feeling about her.

When she saw Martha in the arms of someone else, it confused her as to why she hadn't been overly upset about the relationship ending. Maybe it was her feelings for Jamie, she thought. It had been so easy to forget Martha when she was in her company. She was just feeling so angry that Martha had not spoken to her, before jumping into bed with another woman.

'So, this Martha woman has broken your heart, yeah?'

'No, that's the sad point. She hasn't. I was just kidding myself that we could be together as a couple. It had never been love between us. Just sex.'

Jamie looked at her. She wasn't sure whether she meant the remark or if it was her anger talking.

'Well, all I have to say is that it's her loss.'

Heather welcomed the comment from Jamie and agreed with it. Martha would end up dying a lonely old woman with an aged sex drive if she carried on. Surely the woman needed some stability. Heather would not forgive her for this. There was no way she would be treated like that after they had promised to commit.

This was a different situation from before. They had both known the score. Heather was getting too tired of having to work out whether she had just been Martha's nurse or truly the one she had wanted to spend the rest of her life with. The girls decided not to talk about Martha anymore and finished their coffee.

After putting the world to rights, and feeling as comfortable as ever in each other's company, it was getting late, and time to put the kids to bed. Jamie gave Heather the option of waiting until she had sorted them out or going home. Heather chose the latter. She could see that Jamie needed to keep to the same routine for them both and knew that if she spent any more time in Jamie's company, she would probably make a fool of herself again. But she had felt, for a split second before she had made the mistake of going in for a kiss, that Jamie had wanted it too. This she would take as a, maybe.

## Chapter Eleven

Karen had identified what was left of Ruby's body. Heather had felt for the woman but had decided to keep her distance. She didn't need to be reminded by the appearance of Heather that Ruby was one in a line of people Karen had lost. It was Martha and Heather investigating at the very beginning when she had lost her first husband.

The coroner's report revealed that the gun had probably gone off accidentally when she was carrying it. The positioning of the entry and exit wound showed that she probably tripped and brought the injury on herself. If it wasn't for the fact that there was a grave sitting next to her, Wesley may have been off the hook. The man was in a terrible state. His wife had taken the kids and moved in with her parents, and his job at the college was now under enquiry.

The last sighting of Ruby had been close to her house. They had picked her car up on the CCTV cameras the same day as the picnic and the day after, driving near her home.

There was nothing suspicious about the journey, and according to police surveillance, Ruby had been the only one in the car.

Chloe had covered up her journey by impersonating Ruby well. There were no cameras on the mountain lanes, so the sightings around town would have been normal activity.

Ruby had told her mother that she would be staying with friends over the term break, but she had mentioned no names. The police had made enquiries amongst the people that she knew, but there were no natural leads for them to follow. Her mother was as clueless as them to learn that she had lost her life in that way.

The funeral was a simple affair. Heather was there on duty, but Martha had wanted to be there out of respect for the child Ruby; the mixed-up kid that had had her innocence taken away by a monster.

The family had been through the wringer and back out the other side. Ruby's mother Karen, had nothing left to give. She wailed at the side of the coffin as another of her babies had been taken away from her. She only had little Ben left now. She would have to carry on, for him.

When it was time for Heather to leave, she rang Jamie to pick her up. She didn't want to be left alone with Martha and her excuses in the back of the squad car. She had already tried to offer an empty explanation when they were waiting for the body to arrive. According to Martha, it was a mistake that wouldn't be happening again. The woman she had been with was an old friend of hers. They used to meet up for sex sometimes. Martha insisted that that was the last time, and couldn't understand why Heather was so upset about it.

As Jamie pulled in, she noticed Sue Evans, formally known as Chloe, from the retirement home hanging around the back of the church. She called out to her, but the woman didn't acknowledge her. Jamie knew that Heather had been looking for the woman, so she tried to get a little closer. As soon as she saw Jamie, she darted out the back gate. Jamie ran back to get the car and drove around the church for a while, but she was too late. There was no sign of her.

Whilst driving back to pick up Heather, she saw that she was arguing with a woman. The woman seemed quite forceful in pulling at Heather's arm as she was trying to walk away. Jamie parked at the side of the road and got out of the car, storming toward them.

'Woh, I think you need to take your hand off her Mate. She doesn't want to talk to you.'

Martha was shocked. She wasn't used to being talked to like that by anyone. 'You need to mind your own business, *Mate*. You have no idea who you are talking to.'

Jamie wasn't put out by Martha's comment at all. She didn't give a fuck who the woman was as long as she took her hands off her friend. Heather may be a police officer and could handle herself, but Jamie wasn't going to stand there and let it happen. It wasn't in her nature. Jamie got right up close to Martha's face; sizing the woman up.

Heather feared that Jamie's bravado would escalate. She pulled her away from having a full-blown fist fight with Martha and marched her back to the car.

Jamie was annoyed at Heather for breaking her stride but had remembered that mothers of young children shouldn't be brawling in public.

'Who the fuck was that?'

Heather rolled her eyes. 'Who do you think it was? And I didn't need rescuing by you, Jamie. You were both acting like a couple of kids.'

Jamie shuffled in her seat. 'That was Martha? Oh, Heather, you can do a lot better than that old twat.'

Heather shook her head at Jamie's inane comment.

Martha stood outside the car watching them. Heather told Jamie to get a move on, but she wanted to tell her who she had just seen.

'Wait until she drives off. I'm not going to be the first to drive away.' She sat back in her chair and stared out of the window at the woman. Martha got into the squad car and put her middle finger up to Jamie as she drove past.

'That was ridiculous.' Heather couldn't believe the way that Jamie had jumped in to defend her. But she had secretly enjoyed seeing Martha being brought down a level. No one had ever attempted that before.

'Listen, Heather. Before your Cagney and Lacey wannabe had a go, I saw Sue Evans from the residential home standing at the back of the church. I tried to speak to her, but she ran off.'

'Are you sure it was her?'

'Yes, that was most definitely the woman who called herself Sue Evans at Sunnyville.'

They drove around the church again, but she was nowhere to be seen. Heather needed to talk to Karen to find out if there had been a list of mourners.

She saw her stumbling out of the church and knew that this wasn't the right time. She was already consumed by grief and half a bottle of whisky. She would take the artist's impressions over to her in the morning to see if she recognises her as one of Ruby's friends.

Heather invited Jamie into the flat. She was still quite annoyed that she had taken it upon herself to be her protector, but had to grab a few things before driving back to the station.

Jamie was also still riled up. Her adrenaline hadn't flowed like that in a long time. She watched as Heather quickly moved around the place, picking up the paperwork she had left strewn on the floor. Jamie couldn't help herself. She stopped Heather and kissed her. She moved them both to the far wall and kissed her again. Heather dropped the paperwork and began to react. She was shocked by Jamie's attention but wasn't going to push her away. She rubbed her body against Jamie's. Her hand was positioned just below her left breast. She could feel her tight nipples pressing against her palm.

The longing they had for each other had taken them both to another level. The flat was beginning to suffer as they knocked off ornaments from side tables in the throes of unadulterated passion. They couldn't get enough of each other. Just as before, the kitchen table had taken a battering as the power between them took hold. Neither girl wanted this to end. This was familiar. It was what they had both wanted, and no one would be getting hurt in the process.

When they had both satisfied their hunger for each other, they lie in each other's arms. Neither of them wanted to talk. They didn't need to. They knew what each other was thinking. It was a perfect silence.

\* \* \*

Chloe needed to attend the funeral. Even though Ruby had wanted to murder her, she still felt that she should pay her last respects. Blackmailing her had seemed like a good idea at the time, but she wished now that she hadn't called upon her old friend. It wasn't supposed to have turned out like that. Brian was supposed to die, and she would get her self-respect back. Instead, he had informed her by letter that he had received a letter from Frankie's solicitor. An appointment had been made regarding the will, and both she and Brian would have to be present. She hadn't replied to him. It hadn't seemed to matter much to her anymore.

She had laid low for a while since the death of Ruby, just in case anyone was sniffing about. She had gone over to England and bought a car with Frankie's dodgy money and signed it in Ruby's name. The dealership also looked dodgy enough, so she wasn't too worried about any comebacks. Her arse had been twitching about getting caught out.

Attending the funeral had also been risky. Seeing that Jamie Sullivan standing there watching her also freaked her out. Her mother Sheila had said some strange things to her before she left Sunnyville, and they had been playing on her mind too.

She was on to a good thing at Sunnyville. Taking a few quid here and there, had fed her habit and allowed her to keep a roof over her head. But she had to leave. People were starting to ask too many questions, and she wasn't in any position to answer them. No, her time as Sue Evans had come to an end. She would have to find a new identity to use, after her little stint as Ruby Lewis.

For the first time in a while, Heather was feeling positive about herself. She was still recovering from her time with Jamie, and the smile hadn't left her face. It had all happened so quickly. One minute she was concentrating on going back to work and the next she was being taken to heights of ecstasy. She couldn't believe that Jamie had changed her mind like that. That argument with Martha had stirred something in her. The heated connection they had between them was still firing sparks. She had never encountered this with anyone else before.

The last conversation that she had with her, as she was leaving, was that they would take it slow. There was no need to rush into anything heavy as they both had issues that they were coming to terms with. But the trouble was, she was missing her already and it had only been a few hours. Jamie had felt the same, and when Heather answered the phone to her, she quivered. They arranged to meet up later, Mikey was having the kids, so Jamie had been allowed out to play.

On the drive over to Karen's house, she had tried to put Jamie out of her mind. She was to be visiting a woman that had lost so many people in her life she didn't know how she was still surviving. The walk up the path reminded her of the time her second husband, Phil Jenkins, had died. That had been a day to remember. She had thought, back then, that Ruby had had something to do with his disappearance. There was just something about that girl that wasn't right.

'Thank you for this, Karen. I know that you are suffering from your terrible loss, and I do appreciate it.'

She had picked up the copies of the artists' impressions and Karen had agreed to take a look.

She laid out the sketches on the table in front of her and watched her reaction with a close eye.

'Do you recognise the girl in the picture?'

Karen gave the sketches her full attention. After looking at the first picture, she shook her head. But the second had triggered something, and she thought that she recognised the girl.

'That looks like little Chloe Fisher. She used to live next door to us years ago.'

Heather took another look at the picture. She was right. She knew that she had seen that face before. Heather knew exactly who Chloe was. She had been involved with most of her family and had known them most of her life.

Karen looked back at the other sketch and saw a likeness there as well.

'Yes, that's most definitely her. She came looking for Ruby a while back. But she had already left for her hiking trip.'

Heather had no idea how Chloe would be linked to Ruby's death, but she would bring her in for questioning about the money going missing. She also needed to know where she was on the Monday that Les Thomas died. Maybe she would ask about the Chloe connection then.

'Do you know where she is living now, Karen? Or anything about her?'

Karen thought for a few seconds about the conversation she had had with her, then remembered that she had told her about Frankie's old property having squatters in them. She then remembered that Chloe had said that she was a critical care nurse at the hospital. Heather would begin there.

She called around some contacts she had at the hospital, but nobody had heard of a Chloe Fisher working there. She had also asked about the name Sue Evans. She figured that she may have been using the fake identity again. But still nothing. Karen also mentioned that her mother was still married to Brian Stanley, the bank manager. He may know where she is living, she thought, and he would be easy to get hold of.

When she got to the station, Shane called out to her. Martha had been asking around her colleagues about the woman she had seen her with at the funeral. Heather was fuming. There was no privacy in this place. She might as well scream her business from the rooftops.

'Shane, don't speak to Martha about me, please. We are no longer in a relationship, and I would rather her not know my every move.'

Shane looked like a schoolboy being told off by his teacher. 'I wouldn't, Heather, you know that. It's Josh Bennett you need to talk to. He was loving all this earlier. He had you down as a cheat without asking for any evidence.'

Heather thought as much. If there was ever a time that Bennett could discredit her, he would use it. The chief had reassured her the last time that Bennett had been spouting off about her, that he didn't listen to gossip.

After apologising to Shane for her abruptness, she asked him to accompany her on the search for Chloe Fisher. Their first stop would be the bank to get an address from Brian Stanley.

When they arrived, he was in a meeting. They sat outside his office and waited. Heather could see Shane bursting to ask about Martha, but she wasn't going to offer any information. Eventually, he couldn't keep his curiosity at bay any longer.

'So, have you been cheating on Martha then, or what?'

Heather raised her eyebrows at Shane. She had no words.

He acknowledged her silence. 'I'm only asking. I never liked Martha anyway. I always thought you were too good for her.'

'For fuck's sake, Shane. Can't you keep things professional here? We are about to make a breakthrough in this residential case. Keep your mind on the job, yeah?'

The office door opened, and a smiling Brian interrupted them. He shook the hand of his colleague and waited until he was firmly out of sight before waving them both inside.

Straight away, his demeanour changed. He knew that they wanted to talk to him about something personal, and he didn't want anyone at the bank to think it was about him.

'What has she done now? I suppose this is about Chloe. The bloody girl is a liability.'

The detectives hadn't had the chance to sit down before the man was shouting his opinions at them.

'She's not my daughter, you know. Not by blood, anyway. She's my stepdaughter and a pain in my bloody arse.'

Heather tried to calm him down, but it wasn't working.

'All the money I have spent on getting her an excellent education wasted. She would rather shove shit up her nose and live on handouts.'

'Mr Stanley, we won't take up much of your time. We just need an address for Chloe. We need to talk to her about a serious matter?'

'I knew it. I'm not sure whether you are aware, but I do have a power of attorney where Chloe is concerned, so you can tell me anything.'

Heather and Shane were beginning to feel sorry for Chloe. This man was a monster. He didn't seem to care about the girl at all. He was just concerned about accepting that she had done wrong.

'I don't feel comfortable about talking to you about Chloe without her permission, Mr Stanley. If I can get an address from you, we will be on our way.'

Stanley had thought that he had a right to know about Chloe, as he had a right to everything else that concerned her.

'I'll give you the address of her flat. But I'm not sure if she is still living there. I sent her a letter a few days ago telling her about the meeting regarding her father's will. I haven't heard anything back from her yet, which is unusual for Chloe as it is all she has been banging on about for weeks.'

Heather looked confused. 'I wouldn't have thought that Frankie had much left to leave. He had bought most of his assets with counterfeit money?'

'This may be the case. But until we find out exactly what he has left, and to whom he has left it to, we will never know.'

Kevin would not be getting any of Frankie's money, she thought. And their other brother, Wayne, was still inside, so would not be attending any meeting regarding Frankie's money.

When Heather and Shane went to the flat, they could see that no one had been there for a while. They opened the letterbox and the smell of cat shit hit their nostrils. They could see it all over the hallway and they were worried that the cat was still in there, so they broke down the door to investigate.

There was a pile of letters on the hall carpet and as they walked in further, the cat ran up to meet them. It was in perfect health. The back door had a cat flap, and it looked as though the cat had just come into the house to do its business.

'Let's get out of here, Shane. We'll send someone down to knock on some doors and see if anyone has seen her. I don't think that I can cope with the smell any longer.'

Chapter Twelve

The day Les Thomas died.

'Come on Les. What are you pulling that face for? You love going over the shop.'

As Chloe put a blanket over Les's legs, it seemed he was not his usual feisty self. By now, he would have taken a swipe at her, or at least given her one of those nasty looks that would melt a lollypop.

'What's up with you, you old fart? You usually jump at the chance for some time out. Tiger got your tongue?'

He looked up at her. His speech had become limited, but she could usually get a grunt out of him, or even the odd sentence. Though today it felt like he was trying to tell her something and the words were not coming to mind. He pointed to the picture he had on his bedside table of his daughter. It was new, and Chloe felt that Kate Thomas had put the photo there to annoy him, more than comfort him.

'You want your daughter to come and visit you, is that it?'

He shook his head and carried on pointing.

'I'll get them to ring her for you OK. Fuck knows why you want that grumpy twat to visit you, though.'

Les Thomas lowered his head and put his hands on his lap as Chloe wheeled him out of his room and down the corridor.

They passed the usual shop that the carers used and crossed over the street. The one that was closer to the Beechwood estate was always a far safer bet. This was the one that she always used, as it had no CCTV.

When Chloe was looking for a safe place to draw money out of a cash machine, she remembered this place from when she was a kid. The shop owner had no cameras but a beady eye for thieves. Chloe and Ruby had dodged him many times when they were childhood friends.

He used to sell alcohol and cigarettes to underage kids, along with the odd treat from under the counter. He didn't want any proof of his dealings, just in case the police came knocking.

The shopkeeper gave her a bag of humbugs from the top shelf and a couple of grams of weed from under the counter. She paid for the lot with Les's card, then parked his wheelchair by the till.

The card machine was at the back of the shop, and she took out the limit of two hundred pounds. It had been the third time she had taken money out of his account, and no one had noticed yet. These shops were known to do their banking at the end of the week, so she knew that nothing would show up on record until then. Anyway, if the police came asking questions, she knew that this shopkeeper had more to hide than many, so wouldn't disclose the details of his customers' transactions. Just to be safe, though, she would make her last withdrawal at the end of the week, then leave the old geezer in peace.

There were a couple of other clients she wanted to fleece before leaving, so still had a few avenues to travel. She would just pace herself and not get too greedy.

The job had landed in her lap. She would have been a fool not to take it. It was a good way to get a bit of extra cash. The type that Brian would know nothing about.

Fooling the woman at the post office into opening an account in the name of Sue Evans was easy. She had done such a good job at disguising herself to match the passport photo. She had even impressed herself.

The story of the abusive husband and the need to get away was also a deal clincher. The cashier had fallen for her lies just like the original Sue Evans did. She had felt so appalled by the story that she even bent a few rules for her to get the account set up quicker. The address she gave was for an old lockup of Frankie's. It was easy to get mail delivered there, as she had a key.

Chloe only took from the residents that had given her grief or the ones that were loaded and didn't need the money. She had read their profiles at the office when she had been on a quiet night shift. Siphoning out the easy targets from those that had regular visits from caring relatives was easy. If she couldn't get to the cash, the next best thing was the jewellery. A lot of the old dears still had rings on their fingers, and some even wore the odd, expensive watch. These were extra gems, as she knew she would get a fair couple of quid from her mate at the pawnbroker's for any old type of gold.

When Les Thomas first went into the care home, his daughter insisted that he would have to keep a debit card with him. She didn't want to be called every five minutes when he needed to buy something for himself or have a haircut. She was far too busy for that type of commitment.

At first, he seemed to accept his new home. But it wasn't long before he was complaining about the staff. He wasn't adjusting to the sedentary lifestyle and wanted to be taken out more.

At first, the carers would comply and take him, but then he started getting handy with his walking stick. Because of this, Les Thomas was then known as a 'beater.' The carers at Sunnyville had their own special agreement; if someone was a beater, they would refuse to work on their own with them. It was safer in pairs, as one could notify the other of any flying object or raised hand. He had hit Chloe a few times with his walking stick. But she wasn't having any of it. She would twist his balls so hard that his eyes looked like they would pop out of his head. It was the only way to show him she wasn't afraid of him. She couldn't just hit him back in case of leaving a bruise. If another carer, or even worse, a relative, saw any signs of abuse, they would question her time at the home. It was always best to keep any reprimanding out of sight. No one would dare look down there for any signs of bruising.

As she wheeled him back to the care home, she thought of how he was when she had first brought him out. Something was worrying him. She hated that picture of his daughter. Chloe had only met her once and had taken an instant dislike to the woman. She was a hard-faced cow that didn't seem to give a shit about her father.

This made her think about Frankie and how she would have reacted if she had had to visit the old bastard in a care home. She would probably have done the same thing as Kate Thomas. She would have distanced herself from him. Not shown any care towards him. And use the time as payback.

It had said on Les Thomas's notes that the daughter was now only to be contacted in an emergency. This was her reason for choosing him. If no one cared about him, perhaps the old beater had lived his life with the same bitter heart that was apparent in his daughter.

After her shift, spoon-feeding the residents in the dining room, Chloe thought it would be a good time to do a final spin of the place.

She would miss her time as Sue Evans. It had become a reason to get up in the morning. Her personality had not been as manic and she had even slept more, with fewer nightmares. Not worrying about herself as Chloe had made her forget her shitty life for a while, and the hold her stepfather Brian had over her.

She went into a few bedrooms and found a few hidden treasures. There were also two purses to be emptied in the staff room.

As she went into Sheila's room, she noticed a gold bracelet on the table. She tried it on for size, then put it back in its place. Helen Rees had informed the staff at Sunnyville, that Sheila had done time for murdering her husband. But a lot of them didn't know the full story, so harboured their own opinions.

Chloe knew all about Sheila Sullivan. The mothers would often gossip about her down the shops. They would say that she was the one that was brave enough to stand up and fight back at her abuser. She had become quite the local hero.

The media dragged up the story again when she was released. There were photos of her leaving prison with Jamie by her side on the front of the local paper.

Even though she could see that the bracelet would fetch her a few quid, she wasn't going to steal from someone who had their whole life tarnished like hers.

As she turned to leave, Sheila came in. She gave Chloe the biggest smile and hugged her.

'How lovely to see you, my dear. Do you know where my Jimmy is?'

The hug felt warm and was one that she hadn't felt from a mother in a long time. In answer to Sheila's question, she wanted to say that she had hoped that Jimmy was in hell, but she stopped herself.

'Hey, Sheila, why don't you have a little lie down, my lovely? Maybe you will dream of nice things.'

The woman climbed into bed, and Chloe pulled the blanket around her shoulders.

'Thank you, Joan, say hi to little Chloe for me.'

Chloe took a few steps back. Sheila had mistaken Chloe for her mother, Joan. Chloe had seen pictures of her mother at her age, and they were very similar, so she could see how she would have made the connection.

How the hell did Sheila Taylor remember her now, though? The old girl had dementia and was always confused, but she had said her mother's name clearly. It must have been from her time on the estate, she thought. Maybe she had been a friend to her mother? There would be no point in asking her. Or even worrying too much about it, but she would make tonight her last shift and be gone by morning, just in case.

'I'm not Joan, I'm Sue, Sue Evans your carer.' Sheila looked a little confused, but smiled all the same.

'Oh yes, of course you are dear.' She tapped her arm in acknowledgement. Then her face became more anxious. With a look of concern, she sat upright.

'Did you know that the woman from his picture visits him at night? She was in his room. I heard her shouting at him. She said some horrible words to him.'

'Oh Sheila, you don't know who I am or where you are, do you my darling? There's no one here with us Sheila. You are at Sunnyville, remember? And I'm Sue, yeah?'

Sheila gave her a look of confusion. 'I know who you are, and I am telling you that there is a woman that comes to see that old man, Les. She climbs in through his window and shouts at him. Sometimes he cries out.'

Chloe didn't have a clue what she was talking about. Sheila then started telling her that she was going to the pictures with Sal on the weekend. They would get the number 18 bus and be there by 6.30 pm. Sheila was vacant again. She looked right through the woman. 'Do I know you, dear?'

Chloe comforted Sheila. Her last comment was enough to convince her that she wouldn't be telling the police or anyone about her, or her mother, if her identity as Sue Evans was ever in question. It had all been flashbacks in a confused mind.

Chloe left Sheila to sleep. But the woman could not rest after seeing faces from her past in her bedroom.

She decided to take a walk along the corridor. It was dark, but there was a light coming from under the door of Les Thomas's room. Sheila listened outside. It was the same voice as before. There was a woman in there shouting at him. She opened the door an inch and peered through the crack. The woman from the bedside photo had a pillow in front of his face. Sheila watched as his body flinched and flailed around. Then there was silence. She closed the door and walked back to her room.

Chapter Thirteen

The day Chloe had finally been waiting for had arrived. The only problem was that Brian was the one to tell her it was happening. She had got a text message from him the previous day saying that she should attend. At first, she thought that she would stay outside and watch who turns up. But curiosity finally got the better of her.

The building that they had been sent to, was just a shed made of corrugated steel, tucked neatly behind the bookies. She hadn't bothered to reply to Brian to say that she was attending, just waltzed her way in, wearing a black headscarf. This way, she had hoped that no one outside of the office would recognise her.

When she walked in, she looked around the room. Brian was the only other person there. Neither of her brothers were present.

The assumed executor of the will, Mr Campbell, was a friend of Frankie's. Chloe remembered him from her childhood. He wasn't a proper solicitor, just someone who had looked after Frankie's interests when he was alive.

As he entered the room, he walked straight over and greeted Chloe with a limp handshake. 'How lovely to see you again after all these years.' He nodded hello to Brian and asked them both to sit down.

Brian was the first person to speak. He had asked Mr Campbell to hurry up with the process. He believed that as there was no other beneficiary present, Chloe would be the only one to inherit Frankie's money, so it should be a straightforward process. He was secretly pleased with this.

'As you are both probably aware, I acted for Frankie Thompson on many occasions regarding his business activities. I have called you both here today to tell you that Frankie had not made a will. If he had made a will, I would have probably been the executor, so I was told by Frankie's business contacts to act on his behalf.'

Brian couldn't believe what he was hearing. The paperwork he had seen looked legit enough, and he knew of at least two properties that had belonged to Frankie.

'Mr Campbell, shouldn't there be representatives for Chloe's brothers here? So they can sort out how Frankie's assets are to be split between them.'

Campbell had thought the answer to this question was completely obvious.

'Well no. It was common knowledge that Frankie had disowned Kevin. So, he was no longer a part of this family and had no claim to Frankie's estate. Wayne is still serving a prison sentence, so I will keep him informed of what we discuss today.'

Brian smiled. This was good news, he thought.

'Mr Stanley, you sent me a letter confirming that you are in charge of all Chloe's finances. So, you will be responsible for Chloe's part in all this. Is this still correct?'

Brian looked over at Chloe and gave her a smug smile. He had been waiting for this. At last, he would get back the money he had spent on her and oversee the rest.

'Yes, Mr Campbell. Chloe is incapable of managing her finances, so I will take sole responsibility.'

Chloe was thinking of leaving. It was pointless in her being there, she thought.

'OK. I'm glad that we have that cleared up. So, as you all know, most of Frankie's business activities were illegal. He had made a lot of enemies within his chosen profession and had drawn up a lot of gambling debts. The people to whom he owed the money to are looking to be paid. This is where you come in, Brian. You need to sell his two houses, then pay what he left owing yourselves.'

Brian's face was blank. 'You can't expect people to do that. It's against the law. I will get the police involved and see what they have to say about it.'

Campbell laughed at Brian. 'Mr Stanley. You have married into a family that has an unwritten obligation to pay back the money that Frankie owed. We do things differently from the way you do at the bank. When a member of a family has debts, it passes down to their families when they die. If those debts are not paid, then the debt collectors will do everything in their power to make you pay.'

Brian scratched his head. 'But that's preposterous. You can't make people do this.'

Campbell laughed again. 'I do believe that they can, Mr Stanley. If you want to stay safe in your bed at night, you will have to pay back Frankie's debt.'

Brian was now wide-eyed. 'Me, it's not my debt, it's Chloe's.'

'Mr Stanley. I have a signed document from yourself to say that you are in charge of Chloe's finances, so it is you, that Frankie's debtors will be calling on to settle the debt.'

Campbell took out another piece of paper from his briefcase and left it on the table. 'The lenders are giving you a month to sell the properties and raise the cash owed. I suggest you begin the process as soon as you can. The actual amount of what is left owing, and the interest rate in which the debt is increasing, are shown here.' He pointed to a figure on the clean white page that, when noted by Brian, nearly had him falling off his chair.

'Well, thank you for your time both, and I wish you well for your future.'

Campbell's job was over. He had done what the debt collectors had asked of him and delivered the debt. The rest was up to Brian.

Chloe had expected nothing less from a man that had only ever given her grief. Of course, he wouldn't have written a will. He thought he was invincible. It hadn't been a wasted journey, though. She had enjoyed watching Brian squirm when he realised that he wasn't getting his fat little hands on any cash.

She would leave all of this to Brian. After all, he was her power of attorney, and things like this were out of her hands. She was incapable of managing her finances. Brian had put it into writing. She wasn't going to argue with him this time, she thought.

Brian couldn't understand what had just happened. He had known customers at the bank that had taken out loans with dodgy debt collectors and they had got themselves into such deep water that they had had to sell their houses. Some had even been hospitalised. His body wasn't built to withstand physical violence, so he would have to do some quick thinking.

He would have to make sure that Chloe stayed with him. That way, he could throw her in front of him if the debt collectors ever came knocking.

He then remembered that he had told the detectives about this meeting, and that they would probably be outside waiting to see if Chloe turned up. He rushed outside to stop them from meeting up with her, but was too late. Heather and Shane were waiting for her.

Chloe went with them willingly. She knew the score the same as Brian. If they banged her up, the debt collectors couldn't touch her.

At the station, Chloe sat thinking of her day. She knew that Frankie would have the last laugh on them all, and he had done this in style. Brian would be broke by the time he paid off Frankie's debt. She didn't see the actual amount, but there looked like quite a few zeros were showing after the pound sign and numbers. She would be much better off in a police cell or a nice cosy ward in a nutter's hospital, she thought. After all, they had diagnosed her as crazy. All she would have to do was confirm it.

She had planned to say no comment for whatever it was they had on her. She had committed so many crimes lately that it could be for anything. She didn't want to admit to something that they hadn't known about. That way, she would give herself time to digest what evidence they had on her.

It was probably something to do with Sunnyville, she thought. That Jamie Sullivan must have opened her mouth and told people she was at the funeral.

Heather had called Sue Evans and Helen Rees into the station to identify Chloe as her alias.

Sue Evans identified Chloe as the woman known as 'Red.' She was relieved that this would be finally over and that she could go back to Dai to draw a line under all the lying.

She had told him what had happened, and he had surprisingly been OK about it. He had noticed a change in his wife over the last year and had worried himself that she had been having an affair. Although the explanation that she had given Dai about 'Red' had been awful. He was so glad that she hadn't been unfaithful. He had given her his full support, and they had agreed no more secrets would ever come between them.

Helen identified her straight away and would be informing the head office that they may be expecting a call from the police. She was appalled that this had happened, and that she had entrusted her resident's care to a common criminal. The relatives of the residents that had come in contact with the woman would also have to be informed and apologised to. This would be the start of a long-drawn-out enquiry, and the one she was worrying about the most was Kate Thomas.

'I've put Chloe in the interview room for you, Heather.'

'OK, Shane, thanks.' She tried to gather all she could on the cases that may have something to do with the girl.

Heather had also tried to put some notes together on where she would start with the interview with Chloe.

There were so many crimes that she could assume that Chloe had committed, and others that she would have to tread carefully about.

She watched her on the CCTV. She was a lot calmer than the last time that she had seen her at Frankie's funeral. She wasn't sure who she was at first, but when she started shouting obscenities, it was obvious it was a Fisher's temper.

Heather remembered the first time that she had seen Chloe. It had been at the time of Craig Lewis's, Ruby's father's death. They were doing a house-to-house investigation. The Fisher's had lived next door, and they had spent time talking to Chloe's mother. Frankie had just been arrested at the time and had gone down for ten years.

Craig Lewis had been found dead in his chair at home from poisoning. They assumed that he had committed suicide, but later a diary had been found with both Chloe and Ruby's childhood writing in it.

Chloe had written about Frankie abusing her. There had been confusion over this, and Martha had assumed that the diary was Ruby's and the writing was hers. This made Martha assume that someone had either killed Craig for the abuse of Ruby or that he had killed himself out of guilt. Either way, Martha had closed the case as suicide, so that Ruby could be spared from all the medical examinations and hours of gruelling interviews.

Nobody had known about the abuse of Chloe. She had just been Frankie's daughter and the girl that lived next door. For years, it had gone unnoticed until the diary had been re-opened when they were now adults. Heather had thought of Chloe then and wondered how she had lived her life since leaving the estate, as nobody had seen or heard of her.

When she went to the interview room, she paused for a few seconds before opening the door. She would have to put the thoughts of young Chloe out of her head and concentrate on the crimes at hand.

'Chloe, thank you for waiting. First, I must caution you, you do not have to say anything. But it may harm your defence if you do not mention when questioned something which you later rely on in court. Anything you do say may be given in evidence.'

Chloe shrugged her shoulders.

'We have good reason to believe that you fraudulently acquired three hundred pound from someone last year, then used their identity to get a job at Sunnyville residential home. Here we are investigating several card withdrawals from residents that were in your care at the time. Do you have anything to say about this matter?'

Chloe replied with 'No comment.'

'Is that a *no comment* I want a solicitor present or just a *no comment*?'

Chloe answered again. 'No comment.'

'We are also investigating the murder of a Mr Les Thomas. He had been suffocated in his sleep with a pillow. You were with him the night that he died, weren't you Chloe?'

This time, Chloe had felt the need to speak. She didn't care any longer about the theft claims. She needed to be out of the way for a while, anyway. But they weren't going to frame her for murder.

'I didn't kill Les Thomas. I would never have done that. He was OK. He had his moments, but was just like a Grumpy Grandad. You are not pinning that on me.'

Heather reminded Chloe that she had recorded her conversation. Chloe sat back in her chair.

'Look, I will answer your questions if you get me a solicitor, but I'm telling you now that I had nothing to do with any murder.'

'So, you are admitting that you took the money and stole the identity of Sue Evans?'

Chloe nodded.

'You need to speak for the record, Chloe. The recording does not acknowledge nodding.'

Chloe couldn't be arsed to comply, so she changed her answer. 'No comment.'

Heather sighed. 'Interview suspended.' She looked over at Shane. 'Get her a solicitor, will you?'

As Heather was leaving the incident room, the desk sergeant stopped her. Wesley had come in asking to see her. There was something that he had remembered about his journey with Ruby and thought that it may have some significance.

'Is there a free interview room that I could use to speak to him?'

The man shook his head. 'Not at the moment, Detective Williams. We have a full house.'

Heather went back to talk to Shane. She asked him to move Chloe to a cell while they wait for the duty solicitor to arrive.

She grabbed Wesley and walked to the interview room. As Chloe was coming out, she heard Heather refer to Wesley by his name. She laughed in the face of the man. Ruby had told her about him, and she had thought of him as a sad loser. It was good to put a face to the name, she thought.

'OK, Mr Wesley. I just need to let you know that I am recording this interview. Just in case I forget what you are telling me, or I don't write it down quickly enough.'

He agreed to it being recorded and began with his information.

'When Ruby was in the car, she had taken a phone call from someone called Chloe. I had not heard her mention her name before and none of Ruby's friends at the college had been called Chloe.'

Heather told him that she understood what he was trying to say and asked him to continue.

'The conversation had been about knocking off Brian. I pretended that I hadn't heard the conversation, but they had most definitely mentioned something about knocking off Brian.'

His news intrigued Heather. Wesley had remembered something that may be a lead. He continued.

'At the time, I had thought that it meant them having sex with someone, but now after all of this has happened, I thought that I had better mention it in case knocking off was another term for killing someone.'

Heather knew exactly what he had meant. And, of course, Chloe's stepfather was called Brian.

She had wanted to ask Chloe earlier why she was at Ruby's funeral after they became *estranged* friends for so many years. She had also wondered how Chloe could have discovered the date and time of it. Heather assumed that they would have probably not had any mutual friends after all this time.

She thanked Wesley, and he was free to go—again. She was keeping the idea of him being involved on the back burner. She didn't like the man. Cheating on a wife was one thing, but cheating on the mother of your children was unforgivable.

She had surprised herself with her last thought. Jamie must have got to her. She had buried all maternal thoughts of any kind within her. After meeting Jamie's two, she had started to think of them as little humans and not just as Jamie's kids. They had their own little personalities, and she had enjoyed hearing the laughter around the house. Heather wasn't sure whether she could cope with it full time but, she had been bombarded by barking dogs and they were noisy enough.

Mr Chalker, the duty solicitor, had arrived and had spent a good hour talking to Chloe. Shane had put her back in the interview room with him and had alerted Heather. Shane had thought of him as a strange little man with an obvious chip on his shoulder. He looked at the detectives with distaste.

'Are you aware, Detectives, that my client here has mental health issues? It's just that no one had suggested an appropriate adult be with her when you first interviewed her. I think you need to strike whatever she may have said to you off the record. The woman had not understood the questions you had put to her.'

He was worried that Chloe mentioning that she knew who they were talking about at Sunnyville, had acted as admittance for the crime. She had also nodded when asked if she had anything to do with it. He would have told her not to worry about that, as it wasn't recorded. It could have simply been a move of the head.

'No, Mr Chalker. We had not realised that there were any mental health issues, as Chloe had not informed us of any.' Heather breathed in and let out a heavy breath. 'Now that we know, we will ask our questions accordingly.'

The man bowed in acceptance. Heather continued.

'Miss Fisher, Chloe. Did you at any time impersonate a lady by the name of Sue Evans to get a job as a carer at Sunnyville Residential Home fraudulently?'

Chloe defied her solicitor and answered 'Yes'.

The man looked at her with pursed lips. He wasn't expecting her to admit to the crime and had warned her against speaking.

'Yes, I said I was Sue, and they gave me a job.'

'Did you also fraudulently gain money from the real Sue Evans before taking her passport and personal papers?'

'No, I did not. Sue Evans gave them to me. I did not steal them. She simply handed them to me in an envelope.'

Heather looked confused. 'Yes, but you had told her a series of lies about an abusive relationship before this. Didn't you?'

Chloe paused for a few moments. 'Yes, I did. But that wasn't what you said. You said that I took the money from her, assuming that I stole it from her. Of that you were wrong.'

Heather thought that this was going to be a long night. She decided to move on to Ruby.

'Do you know anything about the death of Ruby Lewis?'

This had come as a surprise. 'No comment.'

Heather looked over at the solicitor.

'She said no comment, Detective Williams. Please move on with your questioning. I do have other clients to see, you know.'

Heather had hit a nerve, she thought. 'Do you remember having a telephone conversation with Ruby Lewis where you mentioned bumping off Brian? I'm assuming it was your stepdad, Brian, as I know that you don't get on.'

Chalker interrupted Heather. 'You are not supposed to be assuming anything, Detective. Do you have a recording of this telephone call? Is there any evidence that you can show us?'

Heather shook her head. 'No, I apologise.'

'Chloe, is there anything else you would like to tell us before we charge you? It would be best to say it now, as you have been cautioned and cannot rely on something you haven't told us in court.'

Chloe gave her usual reply. 'No Comment.'

Heather charged her with fraud. It would have to do for now until she could get more evidence on her. They couldn't keep her locked up, so had to let her go pending sentencing.

Chapter Fourteen

Upon her release, Chloe had to do a lot of thinking. The news of Les Thomas's passing struck a memory. She had thought that Sheila Sullivan had been talking gibberish, but maybe there was truth in what the old girl had to say.

She had said that a woman from his photograph had been trying to hurt him. She hadn't given it a second thought until now.

Kate Thomas was a horrible human being. She wouldn't put it past her to do something like that to her old man. She would visit the woman. Maybe even blackmail her and make a few quid, she thought.

She knew which doctor's surgery she was working at, so followed her home in the little car she had bought in Ruby's name with the dodgy money.

The woman had stopped to shop, so Chloe hid in the supermarket car park so as not to be seen. When Kate finally arrived home, she was back and forth to the car with carrier bags.

Chloe watched carefully and managed to sneak to the side of the car. As soon as the woman had turned her back to pick up another load, Chloe managed to dart inside the house.

She waited inside the living room for Kate to shut the front door and put the shopping away in the kitchen.

As soon as her back was turned, she grabbed her around the throat, squeezing it tight. 'Are you having trouble breathing, Kate? Do you think this is how your father felt when you suffocated him?'

Kate's body wasn't giving up that easily. She fought against her tight grip with her fingers, forcing their way into any space they could find. Chloe couldn't keep up the pressure. She released her. Dropping her onto the kitchen floor.

Unable to breathe, she let out a wheeze and then a cough, before forcing out her words. 'Who do you think you are, coming into my home like this?'

Kate swung out her foot and hooked Chloe's ankle, sending her crashing to the floor. She caught her chin hard on the ceramic tiles and it split, pissing blood everywhere.

Kate grabbed her up by her shirt collar and began slamming her hard into the wall. Chloe fell back down to the floor, and Kate started kicking her like a madwoman.

Chloe was made of stronger stuff and caught her swinging leg, pulling her back to the floor. She forced her onto her back and sat astride her.

After punching her full force in the face several times, the woman was out cold.

When she awoke, she was tied to the chair. Chloe wasn't taking any chances.

'I hope you don't think that I'm going to beg you to release me. You are not worth the spit from my mouth.'

She waited for her reaction. Accepting that Chloe wasn't going to let her go, she waited a while, thinking of all the nasty things she would say to Chloe. If Chloe was going to kill her, she was going to make sure that she had the chance to insult her and maybe push her off the edge.

Her face contorted in disgust. 'If you think that I'm scared of you, you must be as stupid as you look. Kill me if you want to. I don't give a fuck. It will be you facing charges, not me.'

Chloe pulled up a chair in front of her and looked her straight in the face. Kate recognised her.

'I know you. You worked at Sunnyville.'
Chloe smiled. 'At last, the woman is speaking sense. Yes, you're right. I worked at Sunnyville, the place where you killed your father.'

Kate tutted. 'You don't know anything. You're just making things up as you go along.'

Chloe shook her head. 'Why do you think I'm here, Kate? I know everything. I know how you used to climb in through the window in the night and torment him by saying vile things to him. It would not surprise me if you gave him the odd slap as well. You were seen you stupid bitch. Sheila Sullivan saw you.'

The time before she had killed him, the bailiffs had been knocking on the door, and Kate couldn't take it anymore. She just wanted to answer the door and beat the living crap out of them, but she couldn't. Her whole world was about to crash down around her, and it was all because her lying cheat of a father had not died in his sleep yet.

She had been in his room several times, taunting him. She had made him so scared some nights that he would piss himself and lie there until morning. All she wanted him to do was die in his sleep so that she could sell his house and move on, but he wouldn't.

After a few weeks, there were so many people after her that she had no choice but to fake a few papers and sell his house without him knowing. This had made her hate him more. Then when money started going missing from his account, and she had been asked to top up his payments for the home, she just cracked.

She had already been having a really bad day as the money she got from the sale of the house had still not been enough to please her debt collectors. So that evening, she went into the home and suffocated him with his pillow.

She left through the same window that she had entered and hid in the shadows of the sheltered area. Away from prying eyes, or so she thought.

'So, are you going to admit to me now that you killed him? Or do I have to beat it out of you?'

Chloe wanted to record a confession and send it to Heather. It would be the only way to prove her innocence.

If she got done for withdrawing the money and the fraud against Sue Evans, she would get a couple of years max. They may even let her do her sentence in a mental hospital. But if she was charged with murder, she would go down for a very long time. There was no way she was being the scapegoat for this sour-faced old cow, she thought.

'I'm not admitting to anything, you silly little girl. You can't believe the rantings of a woman with dementia.'

Kate knew that someone had been outside the door that night. She had heard a gasp. She wanted to believe it was just in her mind, but the thought had worried her. This was the final cock-up in a history of cock-ups. She had had enough now.

'Just kill me. I'll make it easy for you. I won't even scream.'

Chloe was getting annoyed. She thought that this would be easy. There was no point in even mentioning blackmail, as the woman wanted to sign her own death sentence. This wasn't Chloe's style. She wasn't a murderer.

She kept her tied to the chair and went into the living room to think. Maybe she could tip off Heather? She would just call the police anonymously and tell them that Kate was a murderer, and that she had kept her from escaping.

This wasn't going to be easy, and Chloe felt that her brain was about to burst.

Money. She would have to try money.

'What if you pay me a nice large sum of cash and I disappear without saying anything to anyone?'

Kate Thomas laughed hysterically out loud. She didn't have a fiver left in her purse, let alone a wad enough to cover a blackmail plea.

'Listen, you. Whatever your name is.'

Chloe hated that the woman couldn't even remember her name. Even if it was a fake one. They had spoken several times when she was pretending to care for her father.

'I have no money. Not a penny. You are either going to have to kill me or let me go. What is it going to be? There is a chicken defrosting on that fucking worktop, and I can't afford to buy another one.'

Chloe looked at the woman. She still hadn't decided. She took a bottle of vodka that was sitting on top of the fridge, went into the living room, and kicked the door behind her.

She glugged down the vodka, curled up into a ball, and fell asleep on the settee.

At 3 am, she was woken by a large bang on the front door. The bailiffs were back and had taken the door clean off the hinges with a battering ram. At first, they didn't notice that Kate was tied to the chair in the kitchen and started taking things from the living room and loading them into the back of a van. Chloe hid on all fours behind the curtain.

When they went into the kitchen, they saw Kate. The two men laughed at each other before picking up the chair with her still sitting on it and placing her in her front garden. They took the electrical things from the kitchen just as her neighbours had come to see what all the commotion was about.

One of the neighbours called out to them to tell them that they had called the police. The bailiff had replied by holding up a piece of paper and telling them that they were well within their legal rights.

As they drove off, Chloe climbed out of the curtains. She wasn't going to wait for the police to turn up, so ran to her car and drove off.

When the police arrived, Kate told them that the bailiffs had tied her to the chair. She would sort Chloe out by herself another time. She didn't need the police for that. She had stayed alive this long, with no help from anyone else.

When Heather heard the news about Kate, she and Shane couldn't control themselves. That woman had made every visit to her house hell for them. Heather knew that she had something to hide but couldn't quite work out what. She must have owed quite a bit for the bailiffs to turn up in the middle of the night.

'I hope they wiped their feet when they went in. She would have gone ballistic otherwise.' Shane had to get this remark in. Kate had turned her nose up, no end of times, to his dirty footwear.

Heather giggled. 'I would have loved to have seen her tied to that chair. I don't know who she owed money to, but I've never known any bailiff to do that.'

'Heather, think about it. They probably couldn't shut her up or get past the door. They would have had to tie her up.'

Heather thought about it and laughed. No one had ever riled Heather up so much as Kate Thomas. The detective's behaviour may not have been that professional, but it was only them jibing with each other. Nobody else had heard.

When Heather left the station, Martha was outside waiting for her.

'Not now Martha. I just want to get home.' Martha wasn't there to fight. 'This won't take long. Can we sit in the car for a little while?'

Heather wasn't falling for that one. It had been a long arse day, and she wasn't in the mood for more excuses.

'No, I'm not getting in the car with you. How many more times do I have to tell you? It's over.'

Martha interrupted. 'OK. I'll tell you here then. I'm selling up. The beach house was too big for me anyway, but without you there, I'm rattling around. I just wanted to say that if there was anyone, I would want to spend my life with, it would be you. But as you know, I'm too set in my old ways to commit to anything. Thank you, Heather, for nursing me back to health and for everything that you did for me.'

Heather was a little choked up. She had had some amazing times with Martha, she couldn't deny it.

'It's OK Martha. I've always known that you and I would never be forever. Give those dogs a big hug from me.'

Heather walked away. She would be lying if she said to herself that she hadn't felt sorry that they hadn't worked out. Especially after years of spending many nights with her. She had to thank her infidelity for one thing. If she hadn't strayed, she may never have met up with Jamie again, and their relationship was beginning to blossom.

They had seen each other almost every day. Leaving to go to each other's respective homes had been hard. Neither of them wanted to rush anything, but they didn't want to spend time away from each other, either.

Jamie had invited Heather to stay over. This had been a big thing for her, as no one had spent the night at her house since Sarah had passed.

They took time out to spend with the kids. They had made pizza and ice cream sundaes together. At first, Molly had been wary of someone else being in the house. But when Heather had listened, when she talked about her mother so much, she warmed to her.

'I knew your mother, Molly. We were friends. She was the most caring person I had ever met. You look a lot like her, you know. You have the same beautiful smile.'

Jamie had heard the conversation from the kitchen. She stayed out of the way, as she couldn't hold back her tears.

'Do you want to stay here tonight, Heather? I don't mind. We can make pancakes for Mama and Ricky in the morning. It would be fun.'

Heather told Molly how much she would like that idea. She promised to wake her up first thing and surprise them both.

Later that evening, Heather had told Jamie that Martha had come to the station to tell her that she was moving on. Jamie hadn't held back her joy at the news.

'So, does this mean that you are now officially single?'

Heather nodded her head.

'So, would you like to be officially not single, and we make a go of us?'

Heather nodded her head again. She had been taken aback by Jamie's comment. There was nothing she wanted more than to be the official girlfriend of Jamie Sullivan again. After all, she had been waiting for over twenty years. And with it being the second time around, they hadn't had to explain anything to each other about their pasts, as everything had already been known.

'There is one thing that I want to say to you, Jamie, and I hope that this isn't too soon.'

Jamie was intrigued.

'I think that I've fallen in love with you all over again. Is that OK?'

Jamie didn't answer. She just kissed her girl and held her tight. She wanted so much to say those words back, but she couldn't. Not just yet. She had felt it, though, tonight, more than ever. She would just show Heather how much she wanted her there. The rest, she was certain, would come in time.

The next morning, Heather made sure that she was up and dressed before anyone else.

When Molly came into the kitchen, she looked as though she was pleased to see her.

'Next time you stay over, Heather, maybe you could stay in my room. I have a spare bed that pulls out from under mine.'

Heather hugged Molly. 'That would be lovely, sweetheart. Maybe we could get some popcorn and watch a movie in your room. Would you like that?'

The girls' eyes lit up. Heather watched her as she stirred the pancake mix. She really was a beautiful child.

Jamie joined them, carrying Ricky upside down. 'How are my girls doing? Have you made enough for us?'

Molly told Jamie that she was making enough for them to have pancakes forever.

'Forever. Wow.' Jamie laughed. The sleepover had been a success. They had made the first steps as a couple and things were going well.

\* \* \*

Heather had a different kind of smile on her face when she walked into the office on Monday morning.

She felt that the weekend had been spent in the company of loved ones. Unfortunately, the smile would be short-lived as she had to pay a visit to Kate Thomas.

When the police turned up at her property, she hadn't wanted to report that any crime had taken place. It was obvious from her wounds that someone had attacked her. Heather thought that she would give a follow-up call just in case the woman had changed her mind.

As always, Heather's company had not been welcomed. She did usher her into the house straight away this time. She didn't want the nosey neighbours gossiping about her business again. She had had enough of that over the weekend.

'Why are you here, Detective Williams? I told that Shane person that I didn't want to make a statement.'

Heather was taken aback by the injuries on Kate's face. She looked like she had been in the ring with Mike Tyson. Shane had said it was bad, but she wasn't expecting this. She had felt quite guilty about the way she reacted now.

'Miss Thomas, you are obviously in a lot of pain. Are you sure that there isn't anything you want us to do? Debt collectors shouldn't be allowed to get away with this type of violence regardless of how much money you may owe them.'

Heather had suddenly realised what all the concern over her father's money going missing had been about. This was also why she hadn't wanted the responsibility of a funeral. Even the simplest of services were so expensive.

'Miss Thomas. I don't know what your financial circumstances are, and I am not trying to poke my nose in where it is not wanted, but there are people out there that may be able to help you in this situation.'

'I don't want your sympathy, Detective, and yes, you are poking your nose in. This is my business, and I will deal with it myself. Can you leave my property now, whilst it still belongs to me?'

The old Kate Thomas was back. Even with her face smashed up like an overripe prune, she was still able to cut you down.

Heather left the house. She noticed the for-sale sign on the driveway and hoped that she would be staying around long enough for them to be able to sort out where poor Mr Thomas' body was to be taken.

She had also meant to tell her that they had a lead regarding the card withdrawals, but thought it best to leave her be for now.

Chapter Fifteen

After seeing what the Bailiffs had done to Kate's house, Chloe imagined that a similar thing would be happening to Brian if he didn't get the money together sharpish.

She would probably have to give up her relationship with her mother now for good. There was no way Brian would ever forgive her for this one. It serves the horrible bastard right, she thought. For all the times that he had put her down in front of everyone. He would finally know what it felt like to be the one gossiped about. Bailiffs didn't care about keeping someone's business quiet. And they would not give up until they had their money at whatever the cost.

Being inside for a while would be the best place for her. She also didn't want that mad bitch Kate on the warpath. She had scared the shit out of her. There would be no doubt in her mind that she would come looking for her. She hadn't admitted to killing her father, but she hadn't pleaded her innocence either.

Chloe was still thinking about striking a bargain with Heather. She could tell her who killed Les Thomas if she agreed to go easy on her about the fraud. The only trouble was that the proof that she had was from a woman with dementia, so would be a hard one to prove. She was sure though, that if the police did some digging, they may come up with more evidence to arrest Kate Thomas.

There was also the case of Ruby's death. There was no concrete evidence that she had been involved. The only lead was the overheard phone call, which could have been about anyone. Just because the names had matched, they would have to prove it, and that would be impossible. But now her name had been mentioned in connection with her. They may start digging. It was only a matter of time, she thought.

Firstly, she would have to ditch the car that she had bought with Frankie's money. The DVLA would have been notified of her death, and her license would have been cancelled. If she was ever pulled over by the police, the check on the number plate alone would lead straight back to Ruby. She had used her license to get the car in the first place.

She was shocked that they had found the body so soon. She was hoping for a long drawn-out search, so she could put herself well and truly out of the picture. Finding Ruby so soon, had caused all sorts of trouble for her. Could she come clean about this as well? What would happen to her? The cause of death had been by Ruby's hand and there would be no evidence at the scene of the crime, as she hadn't touched anything. All they could charge her with was wasting police time as they went to look for a killer.

Heather had seemed quite a straightforward copper, she thought. She was almost an estate girl, give or take a few streets. If she could meet up with her privately and tell her the news, she could take it all back if things went tits up. She wouldn't have been recorded and Heather would have no proof.

Chloe followed Heather for a few mornings and found out where she regularly ate breakfast. After the woman had ordered and taken her seat, Chloe slid in beside her.

'Detective Williams. What a coincidence. Is it OK if I sit here?'

Before Heather could reply, she had taken her coat off and made herself comfortable.

'Chloe, why do I think that this may not be a coincidence and more of a planned meet-up? I've heard you are pretty good at making chance meetings happen. What is it that you want?'

Chloe shrugged. 'Yeah, you got me. I need to ask you some questions completely off the record. If you can help, maybe I can help you.'

Heather was intrigued and not shy of the quid pro quo.

'Go on.'

'Well, I have a friend that might know who killed Les Thomas. The only thing is the proof she may have is in the head of a woman with dementia. If this friend was to tell you the full story, would there be any plea bargain had, if my friend was to be charged with any lighter crimes?'

Heather screwed her face up. 'For God's sake Chloe. We know that we are talking about you. What's all this friend, malarky?'

'I will continue, Detective Williams. This friend may also know what happened to Ruby Lewis and how she came to shoot herself.'

'If you did these murders, Chloe, you will be going down for them. They will find proof eventually they always do. Forensic teams are like magicians these days. They pull evidence out of the smallest of fragments.'

'But the thing is, Heather, I really didn't, and without me, you are never going to find out exactly what happened.'

Heather looked at Chloe. 'Without you? Or your friend?'

She grabbed her coat from the seat. 'I'll let you think about it, Heather. Let me know what you decide.'

She had used informants in the past. It was always a tricky way to do policing. Without proof or evidence, you would have to rely on the word of a crook. And that wasn't always a safe bet.

Chloe's crimes had upset a lot of people. She could imagine the way that Kate Thomas would look at her if she let Chloe off with a lighter sentence. And a woman with dementia. How could she help catch a killer?

Heather went back to Sunnyville. She asked Helen if she could have another look around the place. The woman thought no harm in it and invited her in.

'Are we any closer to convicting that impostor with murder, Detective Williams?'

'Mrs Rees, I shouldn't be telling you this really but, there may be someone else in the frame. Would you know of anyone else that may have had a reason to dislike Mr Thomas?'

She thought for a while but couldn't think of anyone specific. He had upset a lot of people by grabbing at them or speaking out of turn. But nothing to make anyone want to murder him. She made her apologies and left Heather to her investigation of his room.

Heather sat in the room where Les died. She looked out of the window and noticed that Sheila's window was directly opposite. The beautiful garden was in between, with its circular seating and beds of roses. She would take a walk over to Sheila and maybe grab her a cuppa.

Sheila's recollection was quite poor today. She had taken the tea from Heather and thanked her as if she was just one of the carers. The woman didn't look very well at all. Heather called Jamie, and she came straight over.

By the time Jamie got there, she was talking a little more than she had. She recognised her daughter and held her tight.

'Oh Jamie, you won't let that woman get me, will you? She's a horrible woman.'

Jamie was instantly worried. She called Mrs Rees down to meet them. The woman had no idea to whom she was referring. Sheila had had the same carers since they admitted her, and they had all loved her.

'It was the woman from the picture. She hurts people. When's my Jimmy coming to see me? He will sort her out. You can't hit old people and get away with it.'

Heather wondered whether Sheila may have been the person that Chloe was talking about. If she had threatened Sheila, she would make sure that the bitch never saw the light of day again.

Heather pulled out a photo that she had of Chloe and showed it to the nervous woman.

'Is this the woman, Sheila?'

She looked at the photo. 'No, that's Joan Fisher off the estate. She's lovely. She tucks me in and gives me toffees from that bloke who was hurt.'

'Are you talking about Mr Thomas, Sheila?'

Sheila stared into space. 'Where the hell is Jimmy?'

Heather had to get hold of Chloe. She would make a deal with her. There was no way she would be putting Sheila's life in danger.

Heather ordered Mrs Rees to move Sheila for the night and to put her on 24-hour surveillance. She would wait in Sheila's room to see if the woman returned.

It was 3 am. Heather and Shane sat in the dark of Sheila's room at the home. They had noticed that the security light that covered the circular garden had been off and on a few times. The fire exit door that was next to the seated area was being used by the night staff to go outside and have a quick fag. This must be how she got in, Heather thought. Shane agreed but had also noticed that the latch was off on Sheila's window, just like Les Thomas' had been.

At 3.30am, the shifts changed over. A lot of new carers had entered the building. Heather heard the latch raise on the window and someone had climbed inside. Shane quickly pounced on the person and held them on the floor. Heather turned on the light to see Kate Thomas dressed in a black hoody with a scarf partly covering her face. She quickly struggled to get free, punching out at them both, but it was no good. Shane had her in an armlock and Heather managed to get the cuffs on.

At the station, Kate broke down. She had had enough of all the drama. She admitted to bullying Sheila and telling her to not say anything about her to anyone. She then admitted to what she had done to her father. She had been drowning in debt and couldn't see a way out.

Josh Bennet had managed to track down Chloe, and she had given him the runaround. She had enjoyed playing with his incompetence and had got him to write down a fairytale of lies before Heather turned up.

When she read the statement, she couldn't believe that Bennett had fallen for it. She told him that this was why she would always be a better copper than him.

When Heather interviewed her, Chloe told the truth. Well, *her* version of the truth. She had embellished some of it for excitement purposes but mainly it was factual. She told Heather what had happened with Ruby.

Heather found the story so unbelievably bizarre that she had to believe her. She also told her that she would make sure that the judge knew of her cooperation when she was to go to trial for the fraud.

She had also heard on the grapevine that a bank manager was under investigation for stealing an amount of money from an offshore account. Heather had let it slip to Chloe that the name had been Brian Stanley.

\* \* \*

Sheila could now sleep peacefully in her bed. Heather had made sure that Helen Rees would get a security firm in to sort out all the windows and doors. They would also be fitting a new CCTV system that covered all the entrances and exits.

It took them six months to finish the work and Heather was glad that her new future mother-in-law was in safe hands.

Jamie had finally told Heather that she loved her. She had also asked her to move in. The proposal came as a shock. But she couldn't say no to the woman that she had held in her heart since she was sixteen years old. Forever young.

<u>Beechwood Estate Series</u>

Book 1

Jamie's Story

Book 2

The Past Should Stay Dead

Book 3

Back From The Edge

Book 4

A Push Too Far

Thank you for your support.

If you enjoyed this novel, please leave a review on Amazon and/or Goodreads. I read every review and it will help new readers discover my book.

Take Care

Kim x

BV - #0565 - 020523 - C0 - 203/127/17 - PB - 9781739743215 - Gloss Lamination